LOVE AT THE HELM

Written with the help and inspiration of Admiral of the Fleet Earl Mountbatten of Burma...

Much to his annoyance, Captain Conrad Horn, a hero of the Napoleonic wars, must sail to the West Indies with an unwanted passenger aboard. She is the Lady Delora, bride-to-be of the Governor of Antigua – a profligate nobleman whom she has never met.

Amid fierce storms and fiercer battles Conrad and Delora fall hopelessly in love, realising that the call of duty makes it seemingly impossible for them ever to find happiness together. Fortunately when love is at the helm the darkest hours are always just before the dawn...

Love At
The Helm

by

Barbara Cartland

Magna Large Print Books
Long Preston, North Yorkshire,
BD23 4ND, England.

British Library Cataloguing in Publication Data.

Cartland, Barbara
    Love at the helm.

    A catalogue record of this book is
    available from the British Library

    ISBN   0-7505-1645-3

First published in Great Britain 1980
by George Weidenfeld & Nicolson Ltd.

Cover illustration by arrangement with Rupert Crew Ltd.

The moral right of the author has been asserted

Published in Large Print 2001 by arrangement with
Cartland Promotions

Magna Large Print is an imprint of Library Magna Books Ltd.

Printed and bound in Great Britain by
T.J. (International) Ltd., Cornwall, PL28 8RW

AUTHOR'S NOTE

When I was in Antigua a few years ago, I visited Clarence House, the Admiral's House, and Nelson's Dockyard. They were fascinating, as was the beautiful island with its perfect climate, lovely beaches and waving palms.

When in 1814 the war between Britain and the United States came to an end, it had brought nothing but loss to both sides. British Naval supremacy had inflicted great damage in the States and also brought American overseas trade almost to a halt. On the other hand, American Privateers of which 515 had been commissioned, had played havoc with British ocean trade, capturing at least 1,345 craft of all kinds.

Privateering continued on a small scale until the war with France ended a year later, then ceased for over fifty years.

CHAPTER ONE

1815

The post-chaise set Captain Conrad Horn down in Whitehall outside the Admiralty.

As he walked through the arched entrance he looked up at the anchor on the pediment over the four Corinthian columns and thought as he had before, that it was appropriately impressive.

He gave his name to the servant inside the entrance and saw a glint of admiration in his eyes, which Conrad Horn had grown used to, since his ship had docked.

It seemed to him as if the cheers which had greeted him were still ringing in his ears.

'Tiger!' 'Tiger Horn!' 'Tiger!' they had yelled as they lined the quayside and manned the yards and there had been applause and congratulations all the way to London.

It still seemed incredible that he had survived what, as a professional sailor, he knew was a voyage in which the odds had been stacked heavily against him.

And yet he had succeeded beyond his wildest dreams and the wreckage of French ships that he had left behind him would, he knew, be yet another nail in Napoleon Bonaparte's coffin.

He saw the servant returning, but before he could reach him, a man in uniform came out of a door in the passage and gave a cry of recognition.

'Conrad! I was hoping to see you.'

He limped towards him and held out his hand which Captain Horn clasped fervently.

'John! How are you? I have worried about you, but did not expect to find you here.'

'I have been lucky in that they have found a shore job for me, for there is not much chance of my going to sea again.'

'You will hate that,' Conrad Horn said sympathetically. 'At the same time, you are still in uniform.'

'I was afraid that I should be rusticated for

the rest of my life, but the Surgeons pulled me through – or rather it was my wife, who is a better doctor than any of them.'

'That would not be difficult,' Conrad Horn said, with a twist of his lips.

There was silence as both men were thinking of the inadequate Surgeons on the ships who, shockingly unskilled, were little better than butchers and often caused the death of more men than the enemy.

'We are talking about me when we should be talking about you,' Commander Huskinson said. 'You know that you have all my congratulations, Conrad. Your reports have been the most exciting adventure stories I have ever read.'

'I wish you had been with me.'

'I wish I had too,' his friend admitted. 'Only you could have inflicted the terror of those night-attacks along the coast, and only you could have evaded the enemy when you were out-numbered in quite such a clever way.'

They both laughed, for it had been almost a boy's prank by which Captain Conrad Horn had evaded two large enemy frigates in the Bay of Biscay.

His own small frigate the *Tiger* had already created so much damage to Napoleon's Fleet which had been so seriously depleted at Trafalgar that *Tiger* was a marked vessel hunted by every Frenchman and all the powers in Europe they had subjected.

The incident to which John Huskinson was referring had occurred at dusk.

Realising he was not only out-numbered but out-gunned, Conrad Horn had strained his sails all through the night in an attempt to avoid his pursuers.

However they were there the next day to continue the chase and when day-light died again, were perilously near the *Tiger.*

When it was quite dark, as a last resort Conrad Horn had played one of his tricks on the enemy.

He had a tub put overboard containing a lantern leaving the frigates to pursue it all through the night while he abruptly altered course.

When dawn broke the next day the two French frigates surveyed an empty horizon.

'I wish I could have seen the "Froggies"

faces!' Commander Huskinson laughed now, and Conrad Horn laughed with him.

The *Tiger* had not had to run away another time and the ships they brought home as prizes, besides those which had been sunk, had made Conrad Horn the hero of a country heartily sick of war and wishing only to learn of victories.

The liveried servant was waiting by his side to catch his attention.

'His Lordship will see you now, Sir,' he said respectfully.

John Huskinson put his hand on his friend's shoulder as he said:

'Go and receive your congratulations. You are His Lordship's blue-eyed boy at the moment and I will not spoil the surprise by telling you what sweets he has in store for you.'

'I am glad to have seen you, John,' Conrad Horn said. 'Take care of yourself.'

As he walked away he was thinking not of himself but of the difference he had seen in his friend.

The wounds which had been inflicted on John Huskinson in battle had left him pale, emaciated, and very unlike the tall, up-standing man he had been before the battle of Trafalgar.

Conrad Horn sighed.

It always hurt him to think of how many men were not only killed in the battles at sea but crippled and incapacitated for the rest of their lives.

The servant opened an impressive-looking door and announced:

'Captain Conrad Horn, M'Lord!'

Conrad Horn entered a large, comfortable office overlooking Horse Guards Parade and as he did so, the First Lord of the Admiralty, Viscount Melville, rose to greet him.

'Welcome home, Horn!' he said, 'and my congratulations and those of everyone in the Admiralty on your brilliant exploits. We are very grateful to you.'

'Thank you, My Lord.'

Viscount Melville resumed his seat at his desk and indicated a chair in front of it.

'Sit down, Captain Horn!' he invited.

Conrad Horn did as he was told, then waited a little apprehensively for what the

First Lord had to tell him.

He knew what he had achieved should result in his being appointed to a larger ship than the small frigate he was commanding at the moment. Besides, it would take at least two to three months to refit the *Tiger* and make her seaworthy after the last battle in which she had been engaged which had resulted in extensive damage to her bows.

Every ship's Captain dreamed of the sort of ship he would like to command, but very few realised their ambitions, and at this particular time of the struggle with France every possible ship that could be put to sea was being utilised by the Royal Navy.

Viscount Melville's opening sentence told Conrad Horn what he already knew.

'There are at the moment, Captain Horn,' he said, 'over six hundred ships in commission manned by 130,127 men.'

He paused as if to make his announcement more impressive then went on:

'And until this war is finished, every one of those ships are of vital importance in one part of the world or another.'

Again he paused, but seeing there was no

reason to reply Conrad Horn merely remained silent.

'We therefore cannot afford to lose any ship from the smallest brig to the largest three-decker,' the Viscount continued, 'and naturally our most precious ships of all, are those which are new and therefore, most effective.'

There was a hint of excitement in Conrad Horn's eyes as the First Lord continued:

'You will remember,' he said, 'that the *Caesar* was the first of the new English two-decker eighties to be launched in 1793. Another ship, built at the same time, on very much the same lines but with additional improvements which we had learned from the French, became Admiral Nelson's flagship after the Battle of the Nile.'

'I remember that, My Lord.'

'It was on this occasion,' the Viscount continued somewhat pompously, 'that the *Franklin*, a new French eighty was captured, with their Vice-Admiral, and turned out to be so notable a performer under sail, that it was decided to build eight ships to her lines.'

Again he paused and with his eyes on Conrad Horn's face, said slowly and distinctly:

'One of these is ready to go to sea within the next two weeks.'

'Do you mean, Sir...' Conrad Horn began only to be interrupted as the First Lord continued:

'I mean, Captain, that your magnificent performance entitles you to take command of this ship which has been named by His Majesty: the *Invincible!*'

Captain Horn stared at the First Lord.

A new ship – a two-decker with forty-two and twenty-four pounders was very much more than he had ever expected.

'How can I tell you how grateful I am, My Lord?' he asked and knew there was an irrepressible note of excitement in his voice.

'Perhaps you should ask me first what are your orders,' the Viscount said with a faint smile.

'I suspect the Mediterranean, My Lord.'

'Then you are mistaken,' the Viscount replied. 'You are to sail first Captain Horn, to Antigua.'

He saw the surprise in the younger man's face and said:

'We have two reasons for sending you there. The second, which I will explain first, is that you should put a stop to the damage that is still being done to our shipping by the American Privateers.'

As Captain Horn had been away for three years this was news to him and as the First Lord realised it, he explained:

'I expect you heard that during our war with the United States of America, they suffered heavily as a result of the blockades imposed on both sides.'

'I must admit, My Lord, I had not thought of that sort of penalty affecting America,' Captain Horn replied.

'I believe the British blockade brought commercial ruin to many American merchants, and if we are honest, Captain, the Americans had grounds for complaint about the high-handed conduct of Royal Naval Captains encountering their vessels on the high seas!'

Conrad Horn frowned.

'In what way, My Lord?'

'The discipline and our conditions of service in the Royal Navy have not unnaturally, kept our ships permanently short of seamen who have sought better conditions and safety from the Press Gangs on American mess-decks.'

Conrad Horn pressed his lips together.

He had always loathed the cruelty inflicted by the Press Gangs in forcing men into service with the Navy, usually without even giving them time to say good-bye to their wives and families.

He was also aware that on many ships, although not on his own, the conditions were appalling and the punishments brutal.

'I think the ill feeling between our nation and that of the United States,' the First Lord continued, 'has steadily increased during the war with France, and because at first we thought derisively that America with a Fleet comprising only seven frigates and a dozen or so sloops would never resort to war, we ignored the danger of their doing so.'

'I heard of course, My Lord, that President Madison had signed a declaration of war in 1812,' Conrad Horn admitted, 'but it was all over last year and I did not realise it would do us any permanent harm.'

'What we did not expect,' the First Lord went on, 'was large numbers of fast privateers which sailed out of American ports to prey upon British merchant traffic to and from Canada and the West Indies.'

His voice sharpened as he said:

'They have even sailed across the Atlantic, to operate off the English and Irish coasts and as far afield as the North Cape, to harass the traffic to Archangel.'

'They must have had very good ships, My Lord.'

'They did and still have!' the Viscount agreed. 'Their super frigates, faster and better built than ours are manned by more thoroughly trained crews.'

'I had no idea of this, My Lord!' Conrad Horn exclaimed.

'The depredations of American privateers off the coast of Scotland and Ireland, for the past three years,' the Viscount said, 'produced such apprehension at Lloyd's that it is difficult to get insurance policies underwritten except at enormous rates of premium.'

'I can hardly believe it!'

'You will soon find when you are in those waters,' the Viscount said dryly, 'that the American ship-builders and designers have produced ships with such fine sailing qualities that they can out-sail all the frigates and sloops of the Royal Navy, besides the fast West Indian mail packets.'

He paused, then he said:

'Food is essential to this island and that is why the *Invincible*, Captain Horn, must protect our trading routes and rid ourselves of the menace of these independent privateers who have paid no attention to the peace which now exists between us and the United States.'

'I can only say, My Lord, that I will do my best,' Captain Horn said quietly.

At the same time his heart was singing with joy at the thought of commanding a new ship, a two-decker!

He was wondering if this was the end of the interview when the First Lord said:

'I told you, Captain, there were two

reasons for your voyage to Antigua. I have not yet told you the first.'

'No, My Lord.'

'You will sail straight to Antigua because you will be carrying on board the prospective wife of the Governor.'

There was a startled silence. Then Conrad Horn said in a tone that was obviously incredulous:

'A woman? Are you telling me, My Lord, that I shall have as a passenger a woman?'

'She is, in fact, I think Captain Horn, a relative of yours. Her name is Lady Delora Horn, and her marriage to Lord Grammell has been arranged by her brother, the Earl of Scawthorn, who is, at this moment, in Antigua.'

If the First Lord had fired a broadside at Conrad Horn, he could not have been the more astonished.

First because he had a rooted objection, as had all good Captains in wartime, to allow a woman so much as to set foot on his ship; and secondly, because she bore the same name as himself, and was one of his relatives, for whom he had not only a contempt but what amounted almost to hatred.

Conrad Horn's grandfather had been the younger brother of the third Earl of Scawthorn.

The two brothers had fallen out and started a family vendetta which had divided the Horns into two factions.

The fourth Earl had carried on his father's battle with Conrad Horn's father, who had been his first cousin, and there had been no communication between their various families, while they were always acutely aware of what the other was doing.

Conrad himself had always been far too busy at sea, since he was a midshipman, to be concerned with family feuds or what he thought was unnecessary bickering between grown-up people who should know better.

But he had, in fact, once met the present and 5th Earl of Scawthorn when he was in London, and decided he was the type of young man he most disliked.

His cousin Denzil had managed at a very early age, to become one of the riotous Bucks who were despised and decried by all respectable citizens.

Having inherited the title when he was only twenty-two and with it a very large fortune, he had neglected the huge family estate in Kent except when he wished to give wild parties there and spent his time drinking, gaming and whoring in London.

His name was a by-word for noise and unnecessary violence in the Clubs he frequented, and the Cartoonists had a field-day depicting the scandals he caused and the miseries he managed to inflict on almost every woman with whom he came in contact.

Because he was heartily ashamed of the family connection Conrad Horn was brave enough to say now:

'I suppose, My Lord, it is not possible for Lady Delora to travel to Antigua in another ship?'

'As I cannot spare another two-decker to make the voyage, and the only three-deckers we have at the moment are under sail in the Mediterranean, I cannot think of any other way in which she can be conveyed in safety to her destination.'

The Viscount's voice was sarcastic.

'You said, My Lord, that she is to marry the Governor, Lord Grammell?'

'Yes, that is correct.'

'It can hardly be the Lord Grammell I remember being on a Board of Enquiry at the beginning of this century?'

'Your memory is not at fault, Captain. Lord Grammell must be well over sixty!'

Conrad Horn was frowning.

If his cousin Denzil had a bad reputation, so had Lord Grammell, as he had heard from various sources, since the enquiry in 1801 when he had thought him one of the most unpleasant, aggressive and foul-mouthed men it had ever been his misfortune to meet.

It seemed incredible that he should be marrying again at his age and to somebody who must be very much younger than he was.

At the same time, he asked himself what did it matter what happened to any of his Horn cousins?

If Lady Delora was anything like her brother, which she probably was, she and Grammell would make a good pair.

Aloud he said:

'I understand my orders, My Lord, and may I thank Your Lordship and the Board of the Admiralty most sincerely and from my heart for entrusting me with this special mission? I shall pray that I will not fail you.'

'I am sure you will not do that, Captain Horn,' the Viscount said, 'and good luck!'

The two men shook hands and Conrad Horn left the room feeling as if he was walking on air.

Later that night, after he had received his orders and detailed instructions from various departments of the Admiralty and had made arrangements to leave London first thing the following morning for Portsmouth, Conrad Horn pulled Nadine Blake into his arms.

He knew as her red lips were lifted to his that this was what he had been wanting for a very long time.

'Oh, darling Conrad, I thought I would never see you again!' she murmured.

Only after he had kissed her until they were both dizzy with passion did she manage to gasp:

'I love you! There has never been anyone like you and I have missed you dreadfully. I swear I have missed you every moment of the time you have been away!'

Conrad Horn smiled a little mockingly.

At the same time he wasted no words but lifting her in his arms carried her from her Boudoir into the large luxurious bedroom that opened out of it.

It was nearly two hours later before they were able to talk, and lying back against the softness of Nadine's lace-trimmed pillows with her dark hair against his shoulder Conrad asked:

'I suppose you have been misbehaving yourself as usual?'

'If I have it was your fault for leaving me for so long,' she replied, 'and, darling, wonderful Conrad, there has never been a lover as good as you. If you had stayed with me I would never have looked at another man.'

'That is one of your illusions which at the moment we both want to believe,' Conrad said, 'and it is therefore perhaps a good thing that I am leaving tomorrow morning.'

Nadine started and exclaimed:

'Tomorrow! But it cannot be true! After two years the Admiralty must give you some proper leave.'

'Instead they have given me a new ship – a two-decker – the *Invincible!*'

Nadine gave a little cry.

'Oh, Conrad, I am glad! I know there is nothing that would please you more. But what about me?'

'What about you?' Conrad enquired. 'I am told that you have an army of admirers.'

'Who told you that?' Nadine asked defensively.

Conrad Horn laughed.

'My dear, you are far too beautiful and too notable not to be talked about.'

'Are you jealous?'

'Would it matter if I were?'

'I want you! I want you more than I have ever wanted any other man! Does that mean nothing to you?'

'It means everything you want it to mean,' Conrad answered, 'and if I were here I

26

concede that I might be aggressive to anyone else on whom you bestowed your favours. So I must commend the Admiralty on their wisdom in sending me away so quickly.'

'When do you sail?'

'In fourteen days.'

'Very well,' Nadine said, 'in that case I am coming with you for at least half of that time. After that you will be too busy to think of anything except your ship.'

'I think it would be a mistake...' Conrad began.

But Nadine's arms were round his neck, pulling his head down to hers, and what he had been about to say was silenced by her lips.

He knew she was right and that after two years at sea he deserved a holiday and the sort of holiday which only Nadine could give him.

He remembered how, when her husband had been killed in action, on the orders of the Captain of the ship in which he was serving, he had been sent to console several of the women widowed in the battle, by telling them of the bravery with which their husbands had died.

As soon as he saw Nadine Blake, Conrad Horn had thought her the most attractive woman he had ever seen in his life.

Her hair was dark and her eyes were green with gold lights in them and they slanted upwards in a manner that was both exotic and alluring.

She had a white skin, a perfect figure, and the sort of seductive manner of speaking which he found fascinating.

He was well aware before he called on her, that the marriage from her husband's point of view, had not been a perfect one.

George Blake had been one of the officers who was always over-eager to go ashore in search of feminine companionship in every port at which they called.

He would come back to the ship elated by some new conquest, wanting to talk of his amatory successes, and it was in fact, a long time before Conrad Horn was even aware that he was married.

He had known by the manner in which Nadine spoke of her husband's death that she was not in the least broken-hearted or even upset.

He gathered that unlike most officers' wives she was not in need of money, and he also learned during that first short visit that her family were of some social importance, and there was a comfortable house in the country waiting for her should she wish to leave London.

That she did not do so, he learnt a year later when Nadine was talked about as being the most attractive woman in a city filled with them.

At first he had not understood the knowing glances, the secretive smiles, the nods and winks that accompanied any conversation about her.

When the truth dawned on him he had made it his business to see her during his next leave.

He had been promoted to serve on a larger frigate and was accorded three weeks leave before he was required to report for duty.

On an impulse, thinking perhaps he might be snubbed for doing so, Conrad Horn had called on Nadine.

She had greeted him literally with open arms and for three weeks she was not at home to her other admirers, nor did Conrad have time to see any of his friends.

Their desire for each other was fiery, demanding and irresistible and it was only when he was forced to join his ship that Conrad realised wisely that fire could not burn so fiercely for long.

'Why must you leave me? Why must you go when we are so happy together?' Nadine had wailed.

He knew even as she protested when he had left her, that she would return immediately to being the social success she had been before his arrival.

There were a dozen men waiting to walk in through the door as soon as he had walked out of it.

Nevertheless it had been a comfort in the long, gruelling and at times, desperately trying years that lay ahead to know that when he returned, if he was fortunate enough to do so, Nadine would be there.

There was something between them, he felt, that was not love but a magnetism which drew them towards each other and ignited a blaze that it was impossible to resist, and equally impossible to quench.

He had seen her once again for a brief three days before he had taken over the command of the *Tiger* and now when he came to her tonight he had known that the attraction they had for each other was still as violent as it had been five years ago.

'I think you are even more beautiful than you were when I first saw you,' he said now reflectively.

'Do you really think so?' Nadine asked. 'Sometimes I feel I am getting old.'

'At twenty-five?'

'Perhaps I have a few more years,' she conceded.

'You could stop burning the candles at both ends and last very much longer.'

'How could either of us ever be cautious, calculating?' she enquired. 'We are both adventurous, impulsive, expensive, and I will never regret it.'

What she had said was true, Conrad thought, and he enjoyed feeling that life was a wild adventure and that if he was killed tomorrow no-one could say that he had missed any of the opportunities that had been open to him.

'Perhaps you would be wise,' he said quietly, 'to marry while there are plenty of men to place their hearts and their coronets at your feet.'

Nadine gave a little laugh.

'They may place their hearts there,' she said, 'but a great number are very stingy when it comes to offering me their names, and I have long ago decided that marriage is not for me.'

'It should be,' Conrad insisted. 'A woman needs a husband to look after her.'

'And a man a wife?'

She felt the shudder Conrad gave against her bare body and laughed.

'I know you would hate quiet domesticity,' she said, 'and being tied to one woman.'

'As it happens, I have been tied to you for the last five years.'

'Is that really true?'

'It is true, although I know I can hardly take much credit for such constancy since the opportunity of meeting women who attract me have been few and far between.'

Nadine knew this was what she expected.

Conrad was too fastidious to entertain for one moment having anything to do with the type of woman whose favours could be bought in any foreign port.

'You are so attractive, my dearest, most adorable lover,' she said. 'But one day you will want a son— What man does not? – to carry on your name. Then you will marry some nice, smug, respectable young woman, while I...'

She made a little gesture with her hands.

'...will burn out both ends of my little candle and when they meet that will be the end.'

'Not until I come back from the West Indies,' Conrad said.

'I might wait as long as that,' Nadine answered.

Then as she laughed up at him he was kissing her again.

Kissing her violently, demandingly, passionately, as if he must make up for what he knew would be long restless nights at sea when the moon and the stars overhead

would make him long for the softness of a
woman and the fire that Nadine could ignite
so easily.

During the long journey to Portsmouth the
following morning in a post-chaise which
despite good horses, was badly sprung,
Conrad Horn was half-asleep.

But while he was physically exhausted, his
brain was active and not in the least
fatigued.

In fact, stimulated by what lay ahead he
was thinking excitedly of the *Invincible* and
what he must do on arrival.

What annoyed Conrad was the knowledge
that he must give up his accommodation on
the quarter-deck to his passenger.

It was infuriating that some unpleasant
hard-faced relative, to whom he would not
give elbow-room if he had his way, would be
occupying the extremely comfortable, if not
luxurious, quarters in the stern that were
the Captain's prerogative.

On the quarter-deck of the two-deckers
Conrad knew there was the Captain's
quarters which would obviously have to be

allotted to Lady Delora, and two small cabins, one of which was the Clerk's office, the other belonging to the Captain's steward.

He supposed, as Lady Delora would undoubtedly bring some kind of chaperon with her and a lady's-maid, these two cabins would be given over to her attendants.

This meant that he must move down to the upper deck to take over the cabin belonging to the First Lieutenant.

He, in his turn, would move out and displace the second Lieutenant, and so on.

There were only six cabins on the upper deck which meant that the most junior officer would have to move to the orlop-deck, again displacing some wretched minor officer, who would have to double up with somebody else, rather than move into the already overcrowded gun-room or sleep on the gun-deck with the men who slung their hammocks between their guns.

No-one knew better than Conrad Horn the strict etiquette that was observed among the men to whom the ship became their home, school-room, work-room and perhaps prison for sometimes years on end.

And because a ship to be a happy ship, must be worked not only with discipline but with justice, Conrad Horn cursed the woman who was disrupting by her mere appearance, the whole pattern of the ship's organisation.

But it was hard to feel like cursing any of them, even the sister of his cousin Denzil, when he saw the *Invincible* lying in the harbour and thought her the most beautiful sight he had ever seen in his whole life.

She was decorated simply because there had been a tremendous scandal some years ago when the decorations of a Royal Sovereign had cost such an astronomical amount of money that the Admiralty had sworn never to allow such extravagance again.

With the adoption of sash windows the ship's stern had become designed to let in so much light and air that it was jokingly said it resembled a conservatory.

In fact, as Conrad knew, since Trafalgar Admiral Collingwood was an enthusiastic cultivator of pot-plants in his cabin.

Conrad had no intention of having any decorations that distracted either his or the seamen's attention from war, but he would not have been human if he had not realised that his ship, new from bow to stern, was not only seaworthy, but beautiful as only a sea-going man understands the full meaning of the term.

His officers had not yet come aboard with the exception of a few who were busy taking on crew that had already volunteered to sail in the new ship, or had been sent from ships which were being repaired in other dock-yards.

It was only after he had inspected the *Invincible* in every particular and found everything about her to his liking, that Conrad remembered that Nadine would be arriving at the best hotel in Portsmouth as she had promised to do.

Because he was so obsessed with his ship, he almost regretted that he had allowed her to persuade him to let her join him for at least a week.

However if he was honest he knew there was very little for him to do except fuss over the few last details to be completed before they sailed, which were actually not his job but that of the officers serving under him.

Accordingly he went to the hotel and found as he had expected, that Nadine had already made herself very much at home.

She had not been a sailor's wife without realising that small extra comforts and luxuries could make a home out of the most unlikely rooms and in the most unexpected places.

As Conrad entered the Sitting-Room which she had forced the Proprietor of the Inn to arrange leading out of her bedroom, he was conscious of the exotic fragrance which hung on the air and which came from the perfume she used, and also from the flowers that seemed to decorate every dark corner.

Before he had time to look around, before he could even realise Nadine's background, she was in his arms.

Because he could not help himself, he was kissing her like a thirsty man who suddenly finds water in the middle of a desert.

CHAPTER TWO

Conrad Horn began to dress himself with what was undoubtedly a thrill of excitement.

He eyed himself in the mirror and knew that his new clothes for his new command were worthy of the occasion.

His coat was of the finest blue broadcloth, the heavy epaulettes which hung on the shoulders were of real bullion and so was the broad gold lace round the edges and the buttonholes.

His eyes lingered on the heavy gold stripes on his cuffs that marked him as a Captain with more than three years seniority.

He had tied his cravat of thick China silk with a precision which was typical and now he approved the cut of his white kerseymere breeches and his thick white silk stockings, which were the best he could buy.

Then he picked up his cocked hat, the

button and lace of which were real gold, and his gloves which gleamed white against the sunburnt skin of his hands.

He looked around the bedroom to see he had forgotten nothing, then for the first time he thought of Nadine.

It seemed to him that she had left him a long time ago, but he had kept the rooms they had occupied at the hotel because he had not been expected to sleep on board until he took over officially, and it was therefore convenient not to move.

He did not realise until last night when he had told the Proprietor that he was leaving the following day, that Nadine had paid the bill up to the end of his stay.

For one moment he had felt angry, really considering it an insult, then he knew she had been thinking of him as she had done when she had left sooner than he had expected.

He had been awake very early one morning because inevitably he woke at dawn. He felt happy and relaxed after a night of love-making, and it was pleasant to feel the softness and fragrance of Nadine still close against him.

Then as his mind slipped away to his ship, the voyage that lay ahead of him and the Privateers whom he intended to capture, he realised that she too was awake and automatically his arm went round her.

'I did not want to wake you,' he said, wondering how he had managed to do so.

'I want to be awake,' she replied, 'because I cannot bear to miss even a moment of you and I am leaving today.'

'Leaving?' he exclaimed in surprise. 'Why? You have only been with me for four days.'

'Four very wonderful days and nights,' Nadine said softly, 'but, darling Conrad, I am growing jealous and that is something I never allow myself to be.'

'Jealous?' he questioned in surprise.

Nadine gave a little laugh.

'I can stand up to any woman and defeat her, but you are obsessed by someone so adorable, so captivating that I have no chance.'

There was no need to explain what she meant, but when Conrad would have protested she put her fingers against his lips to silence him.

'Do not trouble to lie, my wonderful man,' she said. 'Invincible by name, Invincible by nature, she already possesses you!'

Feeling for the moment embarrassed Conrad merely kissed the softness of Nadine's forehead, but she went on ruminatingly:

'When we were in London I possessed three-quarters of your mind and the whole of your body. Now I still possess your body, but although I find it irresistible, it is not enough.'

'So you are determined to leave me?' Conrad said and tried as he spoke not to feel it was almost a relief.

'Prince Ivan has sent his carriage for me drawn by four superb horses. You really must see them!' Nadine replied. 'I am also to have four out-riders, and so that I shall not be cold, he has included a cape of the finest sables I have ever seen!'

'So I should be jealous.'

Conrad put his fingers under her chin and turned her face up to his.

She was very alluring, even in the pale

light of the dawn, and when he looked at her slanting eyes, her provocative lips and the heavy waves of her dark hair, he could understand why there would always be men and more men ready to give her anything she desired.

The look in her eyes was very soft as she said:

'You know there is no need for jealousy, and when you come back with more triumphs, more glory than you have already, I shall always be there.'

'You spoil me,' Conrad said, 'and you know how much you mean to me.'

He spoke ardently but Nadine laughed.

'Not as much as another much larger woman whose name I am always expecting to hear on your lips even when you are making love to me.'

'If I called you by any other name than your own,' Conrad said, 'it would not be *Invincible* but "Incomparable"! There is no-one like you, Nadine, and no-one who has ever given me so much happiness as I have had these past four days.'

'Thank you,' Nadine said simply, 'and

there is always the future of which I shall be thinking as the Prince's horses carry me back to London.'

She gave a little sigh, then in a different voice she murmured:

'But why should we waste the present?'

As she spoke she lifted her lips and as Conrad took possession of her he knew that for the next few moments at any rate he would not be thinking of the *Invincible*.

But when Nadine had gone it had been impossible to think of anything else.

There were still many things to do and every day he found more important details that had to be seen to until sometimes he was afraid they would not be ready to leave on the day appointed.

But yesterday everything seemed to swing into place at the last moment.

The food and water came aboard, the last hammock was slung on the gun-deck, and with a feeling of deep satisfaction Conrad Horn realised that he had his full complement of seamen without one of them being forced to serve by a Press Gang.

Almost the entire crew of the *Tiger* had

signed on, and there were men who had served with him on other ships and others who were determined, because of his reputation, to be under his command.

There were also a few, mostly more experienced, who thought that the war would not last much longer and when inevitably the majority of ships would be laid-up, the newest built would be kept in commission.

Whatever the reasons, the ship's complement was formed and waiting for their Captain to take them to sea.

The only thing that spoilt the prospect, in fact the only 'fly in the ointment', was the idea of starting his ship's maiden voyage with a woman aboard and a woman he already loathed because she was one of his relatives.

He wondered when he had the time to think about it, how old she was likely to be, and decided that as his cousin Denzil was two years younger than himself, that would make him thirty-one, his sister was therefore likely to be in her late twenties.

It seemed strange that she had not

married, except that if she was as unprepossessing and unpleasant as her brother, it was obvious that no man had been fool enough to take her on.

Conrad had inspected his own quarters and decided that they were too good for any woman, and especially Lady Delora.

They were sparsely furnished, as any luxurious items were expected to be provided by the Captain himself, but the table that occupied a large amount of room in one cabin could easily seat twelve.

It made Conrad almost grind his teeth to think that he would not be able to entertain more than six officers in the First Lieutenant's Cabin which he had had to commandeer for his own use.

Then he told himself that the restrictions imposed upon him by his female guest could not last for more than twenty-five to thirty days.

Once he had set her down in Antigua to marry the Governor, he would be able to arrange the cabin to his liking.

In fact, while he complained, the Commander's Cabin was bigger and far more comfortable than any cabin he had occupied in the past.

A frigate was always unpleasantly cramped for anyone as large as he was and it was a delight in itself to be able to walk about the *Invincible* without having to bow his head or, if he was not cautious, to bash his brains on an oak beam.

Conrad, with a last look round the room, proceeded downstairs to where rather touchingly he found almost the whole staff of the hotel waiting to say good-bye and to wish him luck.

'It's been a great privilege to have you stay with us, Captain,' the Proprietor said so sincerely that it was impossible to doubt that he spoke the truth.

The maids in their mob-caps curtsied and the waiters and pot-boys shook his hand.

There was a hired carriage waiting for him outside and instinctively he felt as if he was leaving his old life behind and starting a new one.

It was a cold day with a blustery wind coming from the sea.

As it had rained all night and the streets

were thick with mud, the horses were forced to proceed slowly towards the harbour.

Conrad was thinking that in a few seconds he would have his first glimpse of the masts of the *Invincible* and hoping that 'this damned woman', as he called her in his mind, would not be late in arriving because he wanted to leave on the dawn tide.

That meant it would be best to be anchored further out in the harbour.

He was surprised to see, despite the fact that it was still early in the morning and very cold, there was quite a crowd waiting to see him embark.

He found it difficult to remember his new fame after being for so many years, an ordinary Naval Officer whose comings and goings were of little interest to anybody outside the Service.

As his carriage drew up at the quay a cheer went up from the men and women waiting, many of the latter having husbands or sweethearts among the crew of the *Invincible*.

Despite the fact that the ship was as conveniently near to the quay as possible, there was nevertheless a stretch of water to be covered and a boat painted blue was waiting to convey Conrad to his ship.

When he came aboard they piped the side for him as Admiralty regulations laid down.

There was the Marine Guard at the present, the side-boys in white gloves to hand him up, the pipes of the boatswains mates all a-twittering, the Ships' officers waiting on the quarter-deck to shake hands with him in spite of the fact that they had seen him only the day before.

This was a formal occasion and the correct procedure was something the Navy laid down.

It was expected the Captain formally and with due ceremony, should take possession of the *Invincible* by making a tour of inspection just as if he was seeing it for the first time.

Conrad had already learnt the names of a number of the men under his command and was determined before they reached the end of the Channel, to know the names of the rest.

He had a retentive memory and he knew

that by the time they were in the Atlantic he would know how many children each of his seamen had, who was expecting another addition to the family, and which man had already proved himself proficient as a yardsman.

When his tour of inspection was over, he invited his First Lieutenant Deakin who had been with him on the *Tiger* to come to his cabin.

There his private steward, Barnet, had a flat bottomed ship's decanter ready to serve them with a glass of madeira, and Conrad taking off his cocked gold-lace hat, sat down in one of the comfortable leather arm-chairs while Deakin took another.

'I can hardly believe it, Sir,' Deakin said, as he had said a hundred times before in the last two weeks.

He paused and as Conrad did not speak, he went on:

'I expected you would get a decent ship but I never imagined you would pull out the biggest plum in the whole pudding with a new two-decker!'

'We have been very fortunate,' Conrad

agreed. 'But we still have to prove ourselves, although that unfortunately will have to wait until we have deposited our guest at Antigua.'

He thought that Deakin looked surprised and explained:

'We can hardly go charging about looking for a battle with a woman aboard!'

'No, of course not, Sir,' Deakin replied. 'But I understand there are still some French ships left in that part of the world and if we came upon one unexpectedly like, we could hardly run away.'

There was a glint of amusement and also of anticipation in Conrad's eyes as he replied:

'That would be unthinkable! Let us hope that Her Ladyship is not too squeamish when it comes to the noise of gunfire!'

Deakin laughed, and knowing that he and his Captain were both hoping the same thing, raised his glass.

'To "Tiger Horn"!' he said, 'and may you, Sir, and this ship prove themselves to be invincible!'

It was dark and the lights of the *Invincible* were reflected in an uneasy sea splashing against her sides when the look-out on the quarter-deck announced:

'Here they come, Sir!'

Conrad who had been pacing up and down like a caged lion for the last hour, looked towards the end of the quay.

He was just able to discern the carriage-lamps of a large and luxurious travelling chariot drawn by four horses proceeding cautiously to where a boat, manned by six shivering seamen from the *Invincible* had been waiting hour after hour.

'Damn the woman! It is about time!' Conrad Horn said under his breath.

While he was relieved that his guest had arrived, he could not prevent a surge of indignation sweeping over him because she was so late.

He had to force himself not to show his annoyance when Lady Delora was preceded on board by an official of the Foreign Office who, as Conrad had expected, had escorted her from London.

He was a middle-aged man and as he held

out his hand he said:

'I can only express my regrets, Captain Horn, that we are tardy in reaching you. We had a series of mishaps on the journey, but I hope we have not delayed you over long.'

'I am only relieved that you have arrived safely, Sir,' Conrad managed to reply, hoping his voice did not sound too cold or even sarcastic.

He suspected that the delay was due to the woman who was just coming aboard, and he expected that she had either been late in starting, which would have been typical of her sex, or else had indulged in some temperamental scene which had wasted the time they should have been on the road.

'My name is Julius Frobisher,' the gentleman from the Foreign Office was saying, 'and the Viscount Castlereagh asked me to convey his congratulations on your promotion, Captain Horn, and also to thank you most sincerely for transporting Lady Delora to Antigua in a manner which he is certain will not only be safe, but comfortable.'

'Thank you, Sir,' Conrad replied. 'I am

deeply appreciative of the Foreign Secretary's kind words.'

A figure wrapped in a heavy cloak now appeared beside Mr Julius Frobisher.

'May I, Your Ladyship, present Captain Conrad Horn?' Mr Frobisher asked.

The wind seemed to whip away the words from his lips and as he spoke, Mr Frobisher had to hold tightly onto his high top-hat.

It was obvious that the woman beside him was having to clutch her travelling-cloak around her.

'I think, Sir, it would be best if we repaired immediately to Her Ladyship's quarters,' Conrad said.

'But of course! That is most sensible!' Mr Frobisher agreed.

Conrad Horn walked ahead to lead the way and the small procession followed him, first Lady Delora and Mr Frobisher, then another woman to whom he had not been presented, but whom he suspected to be her chaperon, and lastly a lady's maid, an elderly woman who moved slowly clutching a leather case which was obviously of some value.

Conrad led the way across the quarter-deck to the shelter of what should have been his cabin.

He had only just reached it and stood aside for Lady Delora to precede him into it, when he found beside him a young midshipman.

'Excuse me, Sir,' the midshipman said in a low voice, 'but the Captain of the Marines desires to speak with you, Sir. It's urgent!'

Conrad knew that the message would not have come at this particular moment had it not been important.

He turned to Deakin who was at his side.

"Take over, First Lieutenant.'

'Aye, aye, Sir!'

Deakin, who was never at a loss, followed the ladies into the cabin and Conrad hurried to the lower deck to find out what was amiss.

It was, in fact, only a careless misplacing of the bullets for the marines' muskets which had been taken below but not deposited, as had been expected, in the magazine.

The Captain of the Marines had been

afraid that they might sail without them, and it was over an hour before his anxiety was allayed and the missing ammunition had been found.

By that time, Conrad decided it was too late for him to pay his respects to Lady Delora and Deakin told him that everything was in order.

Her ladyship, he said, had, in fact, been so tired after the journey that she had retired to bed immediately, not even wishing to partake of the meal which had been waiting for her.

Conrad also learnt that Mr Frobisher had gone ashore.

'To tell you the truth, Sir,' Deakin said with a smile, 'I think he had no stomach for the sea and wanted only to get back to the hotel where he has booked a room for the night.'

'I will have to apologise for my absence,' Conrad said.

The First Lieutenant's eyes twinkled.

'I think, Sir, he was so glad to be rid of his charges and for his journey to be at an end, that he had no wish to prolong his farewells.'

'Well, that at least, clears the decks,' Conrad remarked.

He had already given instructions to raise the anchor and move nearer the mouth of the harbour.

He thought as he did so, that if the wind held and they moved out on the early tide they would be well on their way towards the Atlantic before another night passed.

He had a few hours sleep, but he was up again before dawn and as the wind brought them comfortably out of harbour into the open sea, he thought he had never been so happy in his whole life.

He knew that the first days at sea were going to be very busy ones.

There was the crew to be co-ordinated and made to feel they were part of a team, there was the gun-practice which was always of tremendous importance to men who had never worked together before.

And most of all, there was the handling of the sails and making the crew aloft realise that the ship's life and their own, depended on the speed with which they set them.

This was when he thanked God that

Deakin was with him. Deakin had a passion for that kind of seamanship.

He had inspired the crew of the *Tiger* to achieve a record of eleven minutes and fifty-one seconds for sending up the topmasts and they managed to set all sail starting with the topmasts housed in twenty-four minutes seven seconds.

This was the kind of ambition that had to be instilled into a new crew, with far bigger and more complicated sails and with rigging that was likely to be sticky until it had been in use a number of times.

There were so many things to do that the morning seemed to pass like a flash, and it was only when he heard the ship's bell ringing that he realised it was noon and he had not even enquired after his passenger.

He excused himself on the grounds that a Lady of Quality was not likely to rise early, but because his conscience pricked him, he sent his personal steward, Barnet, who had been with him for years, to ask Lady Delora if she would receive him.

The answer came back that she would be delighted to do so, and feeling an uncomfortable moment was ahead of him, Conrad left the fo'c'sle and moved towards the stern.

The elderly maid he had noticed when she came aboard last night was waiting outside the cabin door to usher him in.

Conrad thought with a slight smile that she looked exactly as a lady's-maid should, having a gaunt, slightly grim face, greying hair under a neat cap, and wearing a small, white, starched apron over her black dress.

As a concession to the fact that it was extremely cold, her shoulders were covered in a black wool shawl.

She dropped him a perfunctory curtsy which told him she was not particularly impressed by ships' Captains, but she did not speak and merely opened the door to announce:

'Captain Conrad Horn, M'Lady!'

Removing his hat Conrad walked into the cabin, and looking across to where its occupant was standing by one of the port-holes, thought he must have made a mistake.

There was just a faint glimmer of sunlight

coming through the dark clouds which illuminated the fair hair of a woman who turned at his entrance and he saw to his astonishment, that she was not the spinster he had been expecting, nor did she bear any resemblance to her brother.

Denzil Horn had a long nose, eyes that were too close together, and a face, young though he was, already lined with debauchery.

The eyes looking enquiringly at Conrad were the deep blue of the sea, set wide apart and had a questioning expression in them.

What was so astonishing was that the small oval face and the slim, softly curved body was that of someone very young, almost he thought, immature.

He saw, too, that Lady Delora was very lovely and at the same time, there was an unsophisticated and unspoilt innocence about her that he had never found in any woman and expected least of all to discover in the sister of the 5th Earl of Scawthorn.

They stood for a moment looking at each other and as if she suddenly remembered her manners, Lady Delora curtsied.

'I think we are related, Captain Horn,' she said in a soft, little voice which was not only musical, but which told him she was shy.

'We are, I believe, second cousins, My Lady.'

'Then may I say that, although it has been a long time delayed, I am glad to meet you.'

She held out her hand as she spoke and Conrad took it in his, finding it was small and soft, and yet at the same time, there was a vitality about her touch that was unmistakable.

He flattered himself that he could always tell a man by his hand shake and he elaborated on this point that some hands were very heavy and dull, while others vibrated with the personality of their owner.

It was a contention which had never failed him and he thought, now, that although she was so young, he was certain that Lady Delora had character.

'I understand,' she was saying, 'that this really is your cabin, and I want to apologise for being a nuisance. I am well aware how annoying it must be to have to give it up on your very first voyage in the ship.'

Conrad was surprised that she should be aware of the inconvenience she had caused, and conventionally he replied:

'It is of course, a pleasure, My Lady.'

There was a pause. Then she said:

'I have been hoping all the morning, that you would come to see me and I could ask you if I could see over the ship.'

'Yes, of course,' Conrad replied, 'but I think it would be more convenient if I took you round a little later.'

'Any time that would suit you,' Lady Delora said, 'and please...'

She was about to say something, then as if she thought she was being indiscreet, she stopped and looked away from him as if embarrassed.

'You were about to say, My Lady?' Conrad prompted.

'Perhaps it is something I should not say .. at any rate .. not so quickly.'

'No, I am inquisitive as to what it might be.'

She gave a little laugh.

'I was going to suggest that as we are actually cousins we should not be so formal, but Mr Frobisher was telling me that as Captain of this ship, you are very important and even unapproachable .. or perhaps I am saying the wrong thing?'

'No, of course not,' Conrad replied.

As he spoke, the ship gave a lurch and as she put out her hand to steady herself, he added:

'Perhaps we should sit down. You may find it takes you a little time to get your "sea legs".'

She smiled and walked carefully towards a small sofa which was against one wall at the far end of the cabin.

'My "sea legs", Cousin Conrad,' she said, 'are, as I have proved on previous occasions, extremely good, but I cannot say the same for poor Mrs Melhuish who I am convinced, was sea-sick before we even left harbour.'

'I am sorry to hear that,' Conrad said gravely.

'She should never have come with me,' Lady Delora confided, 'but she is terrified of my brother, because it is only through his generosity that she is allowed to stay with me as a chaperon.'

Conrad said nothing.

He had no wish to discuss his cousin Denzil with his sister and yet it was so surprising that she was so completely unlike anything he had expected that, as if he could not help himself, he said aloud:

'I must tell you that I was expecting some-one very much older, but as our families have had no communication with each other for nearly two generations, I am some-what out of touch not only with the age of my relatives, but even the number of them.'

Lady Delora smiled.

'I remember my father telling me how his father and your grandfather quarrelled with each other. I have a feeling he had even forgotten the reason why the war between them first started.'

'It certainly seems ridiculous,' Conrad agreed. 'But now we have met, Cousin Delora, in somewhat strange circum-stances.'

He was thinking as he spoke, that he was taking her out to marry one of the most repulsive men he had ever known.

As if she knew what he was thinking, he saw the colour rise in her face and a look come into her blue eyes which he had not thought it possible he would see, but which was unmistakably one of horror.

There was a moment's silence. Then she said:

'Please .. I would rather not .. speak of it.'

'Of course not!' Conrad agreed. 'I apologise. I have no wish to intrude on anything that is personal.'

He spoke coldly, feeling his dislike of her brother sweep over him and suspecting that he was somehow being deceived by her appearance into thinking she was different from the rest of the Horns he had always avoided as his father and his grandfather had done before him.

As if he felt that she had snubbed him, he would in fact, have risen to his feet if she had not put out her hand to say quickly:

'No .. please stay. I want to .. talk to you. In fact, I am glad .. very glad that you are here .. and you are a .. relative.'

Conrad would have replied, but she went on quickly:

'I have heard of your brilliant exploits in the Mediterranean. The newspapers said such wonderful things about you, and I felt as I read them that I would like to meet you anyway. Then I knew it was lucky .. very lucky for me that you should be the Captain of this ship that is .. carrying me to .. Antigua.'

There were a million things Conrad was longing to ask.

He could not think why she should have agreed to such a monstrous marriage with a man old enough to be her grandfather, and why when she had every excuse to stay in England because they were at war, she was intent on taking what must obviously be a difficult journey without considering the dangers that lay at the end of it.

Then he told himself that she had warned him once not to be inquisitive and she would certainly not need to do so again.

Because he was keeping a tight control on himself he looked somewhat grim and un-approachable, and this was brought home to him when Lady Delora said with a pleading note in her voice:

'Please .. please .. I did not mean what you .. thought I meant just now.'

'I think perhaps it would be wise for us to forget that there is any blood connection between us,' Conrad said slowly, 'and to behave as if we were just strangers, as indeed we are. Let me assure you that my only wish is to see to your comfort and your well-being until we reach Antigua.'

As he stopped speaking he saw Lady Delora clasp her hands together, and there was an expression in her eyes which made him know that she was pleading with him, almost supplicating him to understand before she said:

'I .. I had hoped that as we are .. cousins we would be .. friends.'

'I hope indeed we shall be,' Conrad replied, 'for the short time that this voyage must last.'

He felt somewhat cynically that there was no chance of their being friends once she had reached Antigua and he had handed her over to her brother and the bridegroom who was waiting for her.

'And .. friends help each other .. do they

not?' Lady Delora asked.

'They should do, if it is possible.'

There was a little pause before Lady Delora replied, almost as if the words burst from her lips:

'Then .. please .. if you are my friend, Cousin Conrad, will you tell me how I can be as .. brave as you .. are?'

For a moment Conrad felt he could not have heard her aright. Then as if he could not help himself, he asked:

'Of what are you afraid?'

Her eyes met his and he knew the answer before she could say it.

'Of being .. married,' she said, little above a whisper, 'to a man I have never .. met!'

Conrad stiffened.

'A man you have never met?' he repeated. 'Then, why? Why in God's name are you going all this way to Antigua?'

'Because .. I have to,' she answered. 'Because I have no .. alternative .. but I am .. frightened .. desperately frightened!'

CHAPTER THREE

For a moment Conrad stared at Lady Delora as if he could hardly believe she was telling the truth. Then he said in a warmer and more friendly voice than he had used before:

'Suppose you tell me from the very beginning what has happened? To start with – why are you so much younger than your brother?'

As he spoke he realised that she was fighting for self-control and with an effort she answered in a quiet voice:

'Denzil is only my half-brother.'

She saw the surprise in Conrad's face and went on:

'But after I was born Mama was never very strong and therefore it was rather like being an only child as I had no-one to play with.'

'Who was your mother?'

'She was American and I think Papa married her because she was so rich.'

Again the surprise in Conrad's face was very obvious and Lady Delora went on quickly:

'I have never met my American relations, but I am sure they were delighted that Mama should marry a man of such importance, and as she was very young, she had no say in the matter.'

'Like you,' Conrad commented.

'Exactly like me!' Delora answered, 'and that is why...'

She stopped as if afraid that what she was about to say would be indiscreet and after a second's pause Conrad said:

'Shall we agree it would be best in the circumstances for us to speak frankly to each other? I want to know exactly the position you are in, and as I am a relative it would not be disloyal to tell me what you are thinking and feeling.'

'I want to do .. that,' Delora answered. 'I felt when I read in the newspapers how you refused to use such cruel discipline on your ship as other Captains do, that you would understand people's .. sufferings.'

'I try to,' Conrad said, 'and if you confide in me, Cousin Delora, I shall try to understand your problems and do what I can to help you.'

He saw a little light come into her worried blue eyes and after a moment she began to speak, telling him in simple words a story which he could easily augment from his own knowledge of the Horn family.

Apparently after Denzil's mother died, the 4th Earl was desperate to have more children.

His first wife had been a weak woman and the treatment she had received from him had reduced her to a condition of nerves and misery which made her practically mental.

When she had finally died the Earl had considered it a merciful release and looked round for a young woman who would give him the children for which he craved, and above all more sons.

He was well aware, although he would not admit it, that his son Denzil already had a wild streak in him and might well grow up into a wild young man.

The death toll among young men who were always taking part in duels, drinking themselves insensible or riding in crazy steeple-chases where there was every chance of their breaking their necks, made it imperative for him to have a younger son to inherit if anything should happen to Denzil.

Although the Earl was immensely rich, no-one ever believes they have enough money, and when he heard that the daughter of one of America's richest millionaires was coming to London he decided that she would suit him admirably as a wife.

As Delora grew older, she realised how unhappy her mother was and how much her husband who seemed to her extremely old, terrified her.

Like the Earl's first wife, his second found it difficult not to grow weaker and ineffective from fear and unhappiness.

Although she fought to keep her health, her vitality gradually ebbed away until she found it easier to become more or less an invalid, agreeing to everything that was asked of her and making no effort to assert her own personality.

'Mama was very intelligent,' Delora said, 'she had been well educated and read a great deal. But every time she expressed an opinion she was either ignored or told she was a fool, so that gradually she hardly spoke to anybody except me.'

There was a little sob in her voice as she said:

'I think I made her happy, in fact I know I did, and we used to laugh and talk together from the time I was old enough to understand what she was saying. But if ever Papa came into the room, Mama would lie back against the cushions and close her eyes as if she could not bear the sight of him.'

Because she was much younger and stronger than her predecessor the second Countess took a long time to die. When she did, Delora had already lost her father, and her half-brother Denzil had become the 5th Earl.

'He had been away from home for so long enjoying himself in London,' Delora said, 'that I did not realise what he was .. like until soon after Papa's death he came back with a .. party of his .. friends.'

Conrad saw her shiver as she remembered them with horror, and as he was well aware of the type of riotous Bucks and the fast, immoral women with whom his cousin Denzil associated, there was no need for Delora to elaborate on what had happened.

It was fortunate that she was still in the School-Room, but she had been aware of a great deal that went on in the house and knew that the older servants and her Governess heaved a sigh of relief when the Earl and his guests returned to London.

Soon he had come back alone and Delora found he was angry with her and learned the reason for it.

Delora's mother had a huge income during her lifetime, which legally was entirely at the disposal of her husband, and she had no say in the spending of it.

Her capital however, was administered in America by the Trustees of her father's estate and when she died they had made it clear that while they were prepared to give Delora an allowance which was more than sufficient for her needs there was no question of any large sum of money being released except to her husband when she had one.

'Now you understand,' Lady Delora said in a low voice, 'that as soon as Denzil knew this he was determined that I should be married.'

There was a moment's hesitation before she added:

'He told me quite frankly that he intended I should marry a man who would share my fortune with him.'

Conrad's lips tightened.

He had always loathed his cousin Denzil and everything he had heard about him, but it really seemed inconceivable that, scoundrel though he might be, he would choose a man of Lord Grammell's reputation for anyone so young and so obviously sensitive and inexperienced as Delora.

'When Denzil wrote to me saying I was to come to Antigua immediately to marry Lord Grammell,' Delora went on, 'I did not think I had to obey him.'

'What did you do?'

'I wrote to him saying I had no wish to

marry anyone I had not seen, and that I thought the idea of my marriage could wait until the war was over and he returned to England.'

'That was sensible,' Conrad approved. 'What did he reply to that?'

Delora drew in her breath.

'He sent a gentleman from the Foreign Office to tell me that as Lord Grammell was Governor of Antigua and my half-brother was my Guardian I had no choice but to agree to the plans that had been made for me. He also brought me a letter from Denzil.'

'What did that say?' Conrad asked.

He knew from the way Delora spoke that what the letter contained had been significant.

For a moment she found it hard to answer him. Then she said in a low voice:

'Denzil said that if I did not do as I was told he would shut the house and .. "turn me out into the street". Those were the actual words he .. used. He said he had the authority to stop me from having any money from the Trustees in America and

76

that all the servants who had looked after me, like my Governess, my maid and my teachers, would go with me and he would not pay them a penny!'

'I can hardly believe it! I can hardly think any man would stoop to anything so despicable!' Conrad muttered.

'How could I let poor Mrs Melhuish and Abigail starve?' Delora asked. 'And the servants who looked after me were nearly all old and would have found it impossible to find other employment.'

She made a helpless little gesture with her hands.

'That is why I have to .. agree to come on this .. voyage. You do understand?'

'Of course I do!' Conrad answered. 'But I have no idea how I can help you to escape from the fate that awaits you at the other end.'

His cousin was looking at him with the expression, he thought, of a small child who believes someone grown up will solve every problem and he told himself despairingly that he had no ready solution, nor was he likely to find one to save her from the situation in which she found herself.

'I am glad you have told me this, Cousin Delora,' he said quietly, 'and I promise you I will do everything in my power to think what I can do to help you.'

He gave her a brief smile as he added:

'We have at least twenty-four days, which was the time Lord Nelson took to reach the West Indies, in which to think, and surely one of us can find an answer during that time?'

'You may .. and I shall .. pray that you will,' Delora replied, 'but I have thought and thought, and prayed and prayed, and all I can remember is how frightening Denzil's friends have always been and that the gentleman from the Foreign Office told me that Lord Grammell is .. sixty-six!'

'I thought he must be about that age,' Conrad said and his voice was hard.

'What have you heard about him?' Delora asked.

'There is no point in my repeating what I have heard at this moment,' Conrad replied.

Delora did not say anything. She was looking down at her hands and he felt in the silence that she was keeping something back from him.

'Suppose you tell me what you have learnt about this man your brother wishes you to marry?' he suggested gently.

'It was when Denzil first wrote to me .. before I replied refusing to go to Antigua as he had .. ordered me to do,' Delora said in a hesitating little voice, 'and I rode over to see the Lord Lieutenant of Kent.'

'And you asked him about Lord Grammell?'

'Yes, although I did not say why I wanted to know. I .. I just asked Lord Rowell what he knew .. about him.'

'And what did he tell you?' Conrad asked.

'Lord Rowell has always been very kind to me, and Mama liked him, so I knew I could trust him to tell me the truth.'

'What did he say?' Conrad persisted.

There was a little pause, then Delora said in a low voice:

'He replied: "Good Lord, child! Why should you want to know anything about that abominable man? A debauched creature I would not allow to set foot inside my house, and I certainly would not permit him to meet my wife or children!"'

'Did you tell Lord Rowell the reason why you asked the question?'

Delora shook her head.

'I thought of asking him to help me .. but I knew there was .. nothing he could do. He disliked Denzil, and Denzil .. disliked him. I was afraid that if he said anything to my brother then I would no longer be permitted to visit His Lordship and I had .. very few friends.'

Conrad was certain that was true, and Denzil's behaviour, if published, would have caused him to be ostracised by every decent person in Kent.

His sins would obviously then repercuss on his sister's head so she would not be invited as she should have been, to take her place in local society.

'I suppose you have been presented at Court. When was this and how was it arranged?'

'Only after I had been told I was to marry the Governor of Antigua.'

'Who arranged it then?'

'The Foreign Office. The gentleman who came to see me said it was imperative that I should be presented to the Queen before I took my place as the Governor's wife.'

'And who presented you?'

'The Viscountess Castlereagh. I only saw her the night I arrived in London, then we went straight to a Drawing Room at Buckingham Palace and I was sent back to the country the next day.'

'It seems incredible!' Conrad exclaimed.

'I think,' Delora said, 'that the Viscountess, and for that matter the Viscount, disapproved of Denzil and that I was to marry Lord Grammell.'

Conrad could see all too clearly that while the Foreign Secretary and his wife disapproved there was nothing they could do to interfere with the private arrangements of the man who had been appointed as Governor.

How Lord Grammell got the position he had no idea, but unpleasant though he was he obviously had influential friends in the House of Lords, and it was certainly not the Foreign Secretary's business to say whom he should or should not marry.

Conrad could understand all too clearly how Delora, small and helpless as any little animal, was caught in a trap from which he could see no escape for her.

The position she was in appalled him and revolted every instinct of decency in him.

But that was a very different matter from knowing how Delora could defy first her half-brother, who was her natural Guardian and bore a distinguished title, and a nobleman who, whatever his reputation, was still the representative of the King with, in consequence, considerable powers in the Island over which he ruled.

Yet there was no point in saying so to Delora, and Conrad merely said:

'Listen, Cousin Delora, to what I am going to suggest to you.'

She raised her eyes to his and he knew there was both hope and faith in them, as if she felt he held a magic wand that could save her when everything ordinary and commonplace must fail to do.

'What I am going to suggest,' he went on, 'is that for the moment, while I am thinking how to save you from your plight, you try to enjoy the voyage which at least is a new experience.'

'It is indeed!' Delora answered. 'At any other time I should be so excited and thrilled to be in such a wonderful ship.'

'Then look at it as a respite between the past and the future,' Conrad said. 'For the moment you have left the troubles you had at home and have not yet reached those that lie ahead.'

Delora gave a little laugh.

'What you are really saying is: "Enjoy today and let tomorrow take care of itself!"'

'Exactly!' Conrad agreed. 'And I promise you that everybody in the ship will try to make it as pleasant a journey for you as it is possible in the circumstances.'

'Suppose we get involved in a battle?' Delora asked.

'If we do, which I doubt,' Conrad replied, 'you must trust the *Invincible* to prove her name, and try not to be frightened by the noise.'

'I am not as chicken-hearted as that!' Delora retorted. 'I think it would be rather exciting to see a battle, as long as you win!'

'If one occurs I will certainly make every effort to see that happens,' Conrad said with a smile.

'After all they have said about "Tiger Horn",' Delora laughed, 'I think any ship which sees your flag coming over the horizon will run away in the opposite direction.'

'You are very complimentary and I hope that is an accurate prophecy,' Conrad said. 'Now, Cousin Delora, I must go back to work.'

He rose to his feet. Then he said:

'I am afraid as there is no sign of Mrs Melhuish you will have luncheon alone but, if you wish, I could invite some of my officers to meet you at dinner this evening.'

He saw Delora's blue eyes light up with delight.

'Would you really do that? I would love to meet them, and I could wear one of my new gowns.'

Conrad laughed.

'There speaks the eternal woman and of course, we would be very flattered to see you in all your finery.'

'Then that is a promise. What time should I be ready?'

'I will tell you that when I collect you after luncheon to take you on a tour of the ship.'

'I was afraid you had forgotten that is what you promised me.'

'You would have thought me very remiss if I had done so,' Conrad replied. 'Besides, it would be better for you to make your tour while we are still in the English Channel. Later it may be rough.'

'I am not afraid of the sea,' Delora said.

There was a shadow across her face as she added almost beneath her breath:

'...only of people.'

Watching Delora making the young Lieutenants laugh and knowing that the eyes of every man at the dinner-table were turned in her direction, Conrad told himself that she was an entrancing child whose unaffected self-confidence would make her a success wherever she went.

He liked the way when he had come to her cabin to escort her down to the First Lieutenant's cabin on the Upper Deck, which he was now occupying, that she had been waiting ready for him, and when he appeared a smile seemed to light up her whole face.

'I am ready!' she had announced, 'and as you look so magnificent I feel I should be wearing a tiara, only I do not possess one.'

'I think it would look somewhat over-dressed on a battleship,' Conrad answered.

He thought as he spoke that the little bunches of artificial flowers that Delora had arranged on each side of her head and which matched those on the hem of her gown were more becoming than any jewels could be.

She looked very young and the excitement of being taken to a dinner party made her eyes shine in the light of the lanterns hanging from the ship's beams.

Her gown was white, but as the new fashion decreed both the bodice and the hem of the slightly wider skirt were more elaborate than they had been for some years.

Because he wanted to pay her compliments but thought at the same time it was a mistake, Conrad said almost abruptly:

'It is cold tonight, and I suggest you wear something warm before we move out of this cabin.'

'I have a scarf trimmed with fur,' Delora replied and as she picked it up from a chair on which it had been lying Conrad took it from her and put it round her shoulders.

It framed her face and her long neck, and he knew with a faint smile as they walked down the companionway which led to the upper deck that his other guests would be bowled over by her appearance.

He had thought when he first saw the First Lieutenant's cabin in which he had ensconced himself that it would only dine six people comfortably and he therefore invited Deakin whose cabin it was and three other guests who were all under twenty-four years of age.

His Lieutenants whom he had chosen himself were a very good-looking lot, and because it had been a privilege to serve with him on the *Tiger* two of them belonged to distinguished families whose fathers had almost beseeched Conrad to take their sons into his ship.

The third Lieutenant, by the name of Birch, was a clever young man who came from a family of ship-owners and Conrad confidently expected him to prove himself an outstanding Naval Officer.

They were all, after their first startled look at Delora when they had seen her going round the ship that afternoon, ready to entertain her and to spend as much time in her company as it was possible.

In fact, Conrad thought with an inward smile, that if he was not careful Delora would prove a distraction which would not augur well either for the discipline of the men or the amount of hard work that was expected from those who manned a ship when she first put to sea.

At the same time, because he was desperately sorry and in a way apprehensive about his cousin, he was determined to make her next few weeks happy ones.

When he was dressing for dinner, Conrad had remembered what his feelings had been about his guest during the last fortnight and laughed to himself.

He had cursed the woman who had taken

over his cabin and disliked more than anything else having to meet one of his own relatives.

Delora was different, so very different from what he had expected, that now he told himself he was already in the position of wishing to protect a girl who was being exploited in an outrageous manner by two unscrupulous villains.

'But what the devil can I do about it?' he asked aloud making Barnet jump as he helped him to dress.

He asked himself the same question when dinner drew to an end and he found himself laughing with the other officers at the table at something ingenuous that Delora had said.

She was not trying to be funny, witty or clever, she was just her natural self and because quite unselfconsciously she said what came into her head, the young Lieutenants found it amusing and her entrancing.

'I was reading in one of the newspapers, Cousin Conrad,' she said now, 'how on your ship you encourage your seamen to play musical instruments, to sing and even to dance. This is something I very much want to see.'

'I am afraid you will have to wait,' Conrad replied, 'until we find out what talent we have aboard. I have in fact always thought it is a good idea for men to play and sing, especially when things are going badly.'

'Or when they are hungry!' one of the Lieutenants remarked who had been with him on the *Tiger*.

Conrad smiled.

He was remembering how on one voyage they had been so long without picking up fresh supplies that the food had become almost uneatable, and only by thinking hard of something else had he and those in the ship, managed to swallow even a mouthful of the biscuits full of fat weevils and the salted meat that was so hard that no amount of cooking seemed to make it any softer.

One of every Captain's incessant problems was how to feed his men with even a passably edible meal when they were so long at sea before they could replenish their stores.

Beer turned sour after a short time and although there was grog – for no ship's Captain dared run short of rum – a man could be flogged for drunkenness which was the only way they could escape from misery into unreality.

One thing Conrad swore to himself was that as long as Delora was on board, there would be no flogging on the *Invincible*.

However hardened he might be to the standard punishment which was carried out with the 'cat-o'-nine-tails', he made every effort not to order it to take place on any ship he commanded.

He knew that seamen expected it as a deterrent, but strangely enough it appeared to have little effect.

At the same time, he wondered how anyone so exquisite and so innocent of the world as Delora could exist for weeks on a ship filled with men of all sorts and descriptions without being shocked and disgusted by some of the things she would see or hear.

He found himself wanting to protect her and to ensure that none of the seamier side

of Naval life impinged on her consciousness, but how he was to do so, he had no
idea.

The dinner came to an end and Conrad
realising that some of his young officers had
to be on duty at four a.m rose to take Delora
back to her cabin.

As they climbed the companionway onto
the quarter-deck she said:

'That was the most exciting evening I have
ever spent. Thank you! Thank you, Cousin
Conrad, for being so kind to me. I am so
very glad it was your ship that was chosen to
carry me to Antigua.'

'I am glad too,' Conrad said quietly. 'But I
cannot promise you such excitements every
night. My officers and men have a great deal
of work to do.'

'I am aware of that,' Delora replied, 'and I
will try not to be a nuisance, but please ..
you will come and see me as .. often as you
.. can?'

There was an insistence in her voice which
told Conrad without more words that she
was afraid of being left alone to think
inevitably of what lay ahead.

'I promise I will come as often as possible,' he replied, 'but I am hoping that Mrs Melhuish will soon be better so that you will have somebody to talk to.'

'I doubt it,' Delora replied. 'She is groaning and complaining about the movement of the ship before it has even begun to be rough!'

Conrad laughed.

'Let me commend you on having found your "sea legs" so quickly. Not everybody is so fortunate.'

'I was not being unkind,' Delora said quickly. 'In fact, I would never be unkind to Mrs Melhuish, but even her best friend would not say she is a good traveller!'

'Which I am sure you intend to be,' Conrad said. 'Good-night, Cousin Delora, and may I say in all sincerity that I am delighted to have you aboard.'

'You were hating the idea when I first arrived!'

He was startled.

'How did you know that?'

'I could hear it in your voice and feel it when I shook your hand,' she explained. 'I was so afraid we were going to carry on the family feud all by ourselves in the middle of the ocean.'

'That is something we certainly will not do!' Conrad said firmly.

He opened the door of her cabin as he spoke and saw Abigail waiting for her inside.

The maid stepped tactfully back into the shadows beside the bed as Delora held out her hand.

'Good-night, Cousin Conrad,' she said. 'Thank you so very, very much.'

He felt her fingers cling to his for a moment. Then as he went from the cabin he heard her cry out to her maid:

'Oh, Abigail, I have had such a glorious evening! It has been fantastic!'

The following day Conrad rose when eight bells sounded at 4 a.m and settled down to the serious work of getting the crew into shape.

The gun-crews loaded and reloaded their guns, many of them finding difficulty by getting used to the new carronade which worked on a recoil roller.

Other seamen were practising the numeral signal code, while Deakin was sending the new men up aloft one after the other until they were no longer afraid of the height or the movement when they reached the top of the mast.

There were also new midshipmen who had come to sea for the first time, white-faced and nervous. They moved about afraid of doing the wrong thing and still more afraid of doing nothing at all.

Conrad spoke to them kindly, learning their names, recalling how he had felt many years ago on his first ship, and how secretly, although he had been ashamed of his weakness, he had sobbed himself to sleep night after night because he was home-sick.

He was so busy that it was not until five o'clock in the afternoon when he re-membered Delora and his promise to go and see her.

He had, in fact, been aware that braving the cold wind and the sleet which was carried on it in sudden gusts she had come out onto the quarter-deck and walked around it, obviously enjoying the weather as no-one else did.

He had a feeling that she would like to be higher still on the Poop where he spent a great deal of his time.

But she was wise enough not to go there until she was invited, and he told himself that would certainly have to wait until they encountered better weather.

He went to her cabin and when he knocked on the door found her sitting on the sofa curled up and reading a book.

At his appearance she threw it down and jumped to her feet.

'You have come to see me!' she cried, 'I am so glad! I was hoping you would remember your promise!'

'I have been too busy until this moment to remember anything but the work I have to do,' Conrad replied.

'Now you are here, would you like a cup of tea? We have some with us and I am sure you would enjoy it.'

'That would be delightful,' Conrad replied.

Abigail who had been sitting in the further part of the cabin now left to make the tea and as soon as they were alone Conrad said:

'You are all right? You have everything you want?'

'Everything except being able to talk to you.'

He smiled.

'I am here now.'

'I am so glad! Please .. can I dine with you tonight?'

Conrad was surprised that she should invite herself before he invited her. Then as he wondered whether to have another dinner party so quickly would be a mistake, he thought of a compromise.

'Instead of my inviting you to my cabin,' he said, 'may I suggest that you invite me to yours?'

'Could I do that? Would it be correct?'

'I am not certain it would be correct either for me to dine with you or for you to dine with me, as you have no chaperon,' Conrad replied. 'But what we can ask ourselves quite legitimately is who is to know, and who is to care what we do when we are between two opposite points on the compass and outside anybody's jurisdiction except my own?'

Delora clapped her hands together.

'Of course! A Captain's ship is his Kingdom. I read that somewhere, and he has complete and absolute command over everyone who sails with him.'

Then with a mischievous little smile she added:

'Please, Captain Horn, will you order me to give you dinner? It would be particularly exciting if tonight we could dine alone so that I could talk to you.'

Just for a moment Conrad hesitated.

He had a feeling that a *tête-à-tête* dinner was something slightly reprehensible from a social point of view, even though Delora was his cousin.

Then he told himself he was being needlessly worried about the conventions and, in view of what awaited her in Antigua, anything she did aboard ship would pale into insignificance beside the behaviour of her brother and her future husband.

'I should be delighted to accept Your Ladyship's invitation!' he said formally, and liked the little chuckle of laughter she gave.

Two hours later Conrad entered Delora's cabin to find the table laid and lit with candles instead of the lantern hanging over it, and he realised from her appearance she had made every effort.

The gown she wore tonight was a very pale blue, but instead of flowers there were two little bows in her hair and round her neck was a string of pearls which he was to learn later had belonged to her mother.

He realised as he greeted her with a formal bow while she curtsied that she was so excited that she gave a little jump for joy and said as if she could keep it a secret no longer:

'I have planned a very special dinner for you tonight, and I shall be very disappointed if you do not enjoy it.'

'A special dinner?' Conrad enquired.

'Lord Rowell told me when he knew I was coming on your ship it would be wise to bring some delicacies with me to augment what he warned me might be a very prosaic and unimaginative ship's menu.'

'That is certainly a polite word for it after we have been at sea for some weeks,'

Conrad remarked. 'But at the moment we have fresh chicken, lamb and pork aboard, and unless the Chef ruins them in cooking, they should be palatable.'

'I was enjoying myself so much last night that I did not notice what I was eating,' Delora said, 'but I must not spoil the surprise by telling you what I have for you tonight.'

It was certainly a surprise, Conrad thought, to eat pâté together with ox-tongue and a goose, both of which Delora told him came from the Home Farm.

'Have you never been to the family house?' she enquired curiously.

Conrad shook his head.

'My father would have had a fit if I had even suggested such a thing! When I was a small boy and heard him ranting against your grandfather and his cousin, I used to imagine it was something like hell, all black with the inhabitants enveloped in flames which flared from within them because they were so wicked!'

Delora's laughter rang out.

'The very opposite is the truth. It is a

beautiful house and I know because you have good taste that you would love it.'

'How do you know I have good taste?'

'I think it is part of your character and your personality,' she replied, 'just as I know you are kind and generous, brave and truthful.'

Conrad held up his hands in dismay.

'Stop! Stop!' he objected. 'You are giving me a halo and making me into a hero when I assure you I deserve neither. I am simply a man dedicated to his profession who has been extremely lucky. Beyond that I am nothing else.'

'Now you are being modest,' Delora said teasingly. 'You forget I have read everything they said about you in the *Times* and the *Morning Post* and I saw the way your officers looked at you last night. Whether you like it or not, they think you are wonderful!'

She paused before she added:

'As I do!'

She spoke spontaneously as if it came to her lips without really thinking what she was saying.

Then as she met Conrad's eyes it was

impossible to look away and he saw the colour rise slowly, very slowly up her cheeks.

It was like watching the dawn break over the horizon as he had done so often in his life, and he thought it would be impossible for any woman to be so lovely, and at the same time unspoilt.

As if she was suddenly aware that he was staring at her there was a strange expression on her face to which he was afraid to put a name, and he pushed back his chair from the table.

'Thank you, Cousin Delora,' he said. 'You should find yourself something to do while you are at sea, such as painting, unless you prefer sewing.'

'What I really want to do,' Delora replied, 'is to walk about the ship and watch you and your seamen at work. Today I was afraid to leave the deck outside my cabin, while I longed to join you overhead on what I believe you call the Poop deck.'

'You have to await an invitation from the Captain.'

'And will you invite me?'

'That remains to be seen. As you must

realise, we are a battle-ship and there is little time for frivolities.'

He deliberately made his voice sound scathing.

'Are you saying,' Delora asked in a low voice, 'that you have changed your mind .. and now wish I was .. not on .. board?'

There was something so wistful and hurt in her tone that instinctively Conrad said quickly:

'No, of course not! I like having you here! You know I want you to be happy. It is just...'

It was his turn to find it difficult to finish the sentence but Delora did it for him.

'...it is just that you do not wish to be too .. involved with me. That is the truth .. is it not?'

He was surprised that she was so perceptive.

At the same time he felt he was deliberately being unkind and he knew without being told that she desperately needed his help and comfort.

He did not answer, and after a moment she said:

'I knew as soon as I saw you that you were everything I had .. hoped you would be .. and when you .. talked to me yesterday I felt .. or rather I sensed that you would help me when I was so .. so frightened, that I wanted to .. die!'

'You must not feel like that,' Conrad said almost sharply, as if he was talking to a terrified midshipman.

'I cannot help it because it is the truth,' Delora said, 'and you did say that we would forget what lay ahead and you wanted me to be happy while we were between yesterday and tomorrow.'

'That is of course what I want,' Conrad agreed, feeling as if he was being driven into a corner. 'At the same time, for your sake I have to be sensible.'

'By that you mean not being .. involved,' Delora said logically.

'Not exactly,' he objected, 'I am trying to do what is best for you.'

He knew as he spoke that what he was really saying was that whatever happened this child must not rely too much on him, because inevitably when the moment came, he would be obliged to fail her.

More important still she must not in any circumstances, fall in love with him.

He did not think it was likely to happen because she was so much younger not only in years, but he was sure in every other way.

But he would not have been human if he had not been aware that because of his looks, his fame, and because he himself had never given his heart lightly, women were often bowled over the moment they met him.

Until he had known Nadine and been more or less faithful to her because she supplied a need in his life which every sailor recognised, there had been a number of women who had pursued him.

While they had tried by every wile and allure known to the feminine mind to inveigle him into the position of a supplicant, he had always turned the tables on them.

They had become involved with him but he had remained whole-hearted and to a certain extent uncommitted.

He had accepted the favours that were

offered him. At the same time, he had known that they meant nothing serious but were as delightful as the flowers on a dinner-table which had begun to fade by the time the dawn broke.

Any *affaire de coeur* in which he had been involved had been with a woman well able to look after herself and who knew that if she played with fire, it was easy to get burnt.

Delora was different, so different, Conrad thought, that he wanted to think of her as the child she had appeared to be when he had first seen her.

He was however, already aware that her intelligent mind had nothing childlike about it, and he knew too that feelings were awakening in her like a rose coming into bloom.

It only needed love to turn her from a girl into a woman.

It suddenly struck him that nothing could be more exciting, more thrilling or more enthralling than to awaken her to a realisation of what love could be.

Then shocked by the idea he told himself that must never happen!

It would be wrong, absolutely wrong in every way, to abuse the trust she had given him and in his position as a relative to make her aware of him as a man.

Besides, apart from anything else, she was promised in marriage and it was not his place to question the character or the behaviour of her future husband.

Even as he thought it, he felt himself rebelling violently at the idea of anything so exquisite and so pure being touched – perhaps besmirched was a better word – by a monster like Grammell.

As he recalled the man he had last heard mouthing obscenities which the roughest seaman would have been ashamed to use, Conrad felt his hands twitch as if they were ready to choke the life out of the man who could debase not only the name he bore, but the class from which he had come.

Then strangely, surprisingly, because he was not aware that Delora could read his mind, he heard her say in a whisper:

'If you .. feel like that about .. him .. how do you think I .. feel?'

107

CHAPTER FOUR

Standing on the Poop deck from which he could observe the sea occasionally spraying over the bow, Conrad was acutely aware of a small figure moving about on the deck below.

They were now ten days out from Portsmouth, and the Atlantic had been at first tempestuous but was now settling down to an uncomfortable deep swell.

There had been no sign of Mrs Melhuish and Delora reported that she had no intention of leaving her cabin until they were in calm waters.

'Which will be never!' Delora laughed, 'because she dislikes the sea and she is praying only to reach dry land.'

This had meant that Conrad spent a great deal more time with his cousin than he would have done otherwise.

He was aware, with a sensibility he had

not expected in himself, how when she was alone her thoughts dwelt on what was waiting for her at the end of the voyage.

He saw when he came into her cabin that for the first moment the fear was vividly there in her eyes before his very presence dispersed it.

When he turned his head to look up at the masts he could see her wrapped in a blue cloak that was lined with ermine and trimmed with the same soft white fur round the hood.

It framed her face giving her an ethereal spiritual appearance until she smiled, when Conrad had found there was a hint of mischief in the soft curves of her mouth.

'She is lovely! Absolutely lovely!' he would tell himself in the dark watches of the night. 'How can I hand her over to a beast like Grammell?'

Vaguely out of the mists of time memories had come to him of other things he had heard about the present Governor of Antigua, things so revolting, so distasteful to any decent man that Conrad was disturbed even to think of them.

Nevertheless he could not banish them from his mind, and when he was obliged to think of them in relation to Delora he wondered if the best thing he could do would be to throw her overboard before they reached Antigua.

At least she would die a clean death in the sea.

Those were his thoughts at night. In the day-time he told himself he was being absurd and hysterical and tried to go on pretending it was not really any of his business.

There was no doubt, apart from her fear of the future, that Delora was enjoying herself.

By now every young Lieutenant thought himself to be in love with her and even the seamen's eyes followed her whenever she was on deck.

Conrad made a pretence of looking at the main mast, but he knew in reality that his eyes wandered downwards to where Delora was walking round the three boats secured on the quarter-deck, and moving with an unmistakable grace despite the fact that the ship was rolling quite considerably.

Conrad had already warned her a dozen times not to go out on deck if it was rough, but she had laughed at him and told him she was a country girl.

'I am used to fresh air,' she said, 'and if the spray makes me wet I have plenty of gowns to change into.'

'It is your health I am worrying about,' Conrad protested. 'These North winds bite into one, and I do not want you to go down with pneumonia.'

'I will do my best not to inconvenience you, Captain!'

She spoke with a smile on her lips, and although he wanted to be firm with her he smiled back and knew she would get her own way.

He was aware now that the wind was growing stronger and the ship began to come alive with a creaking of timber and a harping in the rigging.

He saw that the gusts were whipping Delora's skirts around her and she was holding on to her cloak with both hands.

'She should go to her cabin,' Conrad said

beneath his breath.

At that moment there came a hail from the crow's nest.

'Sail ho! Deck, there, a sail ahead!'

'A sail!'

Conrad gazed upwards.

The look-out was clinging to his perch being swung backwards and forwards by the swell.

He saw one of the midshipmen standing beside him and ordered:

'Up you go, Harris! Take a glass with you and tell me what you can see.'

The midshipman hurried to obey him and a few minutes later the Captain heard his voice calling down to him through the wind:

'I think she's a Frenchie, Sir. I can see the cut of her tops'ls.'

Conrad drew in his breath.

'Man the braces, there!' he shouted, and as Deakin joined him on the Poop, added:

'Beat to quarters, if you please, Mr Deakin and clear for action!'

As the drum rolled the hands came pouring up to man the guns on the quarter-deck and Conrad walked down from the

Poop to where Delora was standing staring excitedly out to sea.

'Your place is below, Delora,' he said. 'Take Abigail with you, and you will stay in a lower cabin until the action is over.'

'Oh, please...' she began, but Conrad was in no mood for argument. He called to the nearest Lieutenant.

'Mr Latham – conduct Her Ladyship and her maid to my cabin and see that they are safe before you leave them!'

'Aye, aye, Sir!' the Lieutenant replied, delighted at the order.

Deliberately because he was worried about her, Conrad tried not to look at Delora as she left him.

Nevertheless he saw her smile and wave her hand as Mr Latham led the way to her own cabin to collect Abigail.

For several minutes the ship was in turmoil of activity as the men began the drill they had been practising almost every hour of the day since they left Portsmouth.

The guns were run out and manned, the decks were sanded, the hoses rigged to the pumps and fire-extinguishers.

Conrad looked up at the sail and said harshly:

'I'll have two reefs taken in those Tops'ls, Commander!'

Now he could see the ship they were approaching quite clearly, and she was unmistakably a Frenchman.

She was flying a red, white and blue flag and Conrad glanced up overhead to make certain the White Ensign fluttered in the breeze.

Then he heard Deakin say quietly beside him:

'She's opened fire, Sir!'

It was a mistake, as every English Captain knew, to open fire at long range. The sound did not reach them and the puff of smoke was blown away by the wind.

Conrad had always believed that the first broadside should be saved up for use at the exact moment when it could do the maximum harm.

Then as the ships drew a little closer a strange thing happened.

There was no more firing, and the French ship altered course.

Conrad waited, then as she turned to starboard he realised what was happening.

She, by now, had seen the size of the *Invincible* and was running away!

'Mr Deakin,' he asked, 'what distance do you think there is between our two ships?'

'Over half of a mile, Sir.'

'Thank you,' Conrad said.

He gave the order for more sail, then watched the ship ahead doing the same thing.

He knew now it was a French Man-o'-War not much smaller than the *Invincible* but older, and it had doubtless been at sea for a long time.

That would account for her not being anxious to do battle with anything except ships smaller than herself whom she could easily out-gun.

'We'll overhaul her, Sir, if only the wind holds!' Deakin said excitedly.

It seemed as if it had every intention of doing so, for the *Invincible* under full sail, was pitching and tossing unpleasantly, but at the same time, she was riding the sea in a manner which Conrad had hoped she would be able to achieve in an emergency.

He drew nearer and nearer to the French ship and now Conrad gave the order for which every man aboard was waiting.

'Cock your locks!' he commanded. 'Take your aim – fire!'

The roar of the broadside coincided exactly with that of the French ship. Conrad heard the sound of their shot as it passed overhead, fortunately without striking a mast.

It was obvious the French knew they could not go on running and must fight to save themselves.

The *Invincible* was enveloped in smoke, and Conrad could hear his First Lieutenant's voice, high with excitement, giving orders.

The guns bellowed, the crews sponged and rammed.

'Fire as you will!'

Conrad heard the order, and the more expert gun-crews got their shots off quicker than the others.

He realised the enemy's returns were now falling short as great fountains of spray rose above the side of the ship and splashed onto the deck.

Then he saw a main mast on the French ship fall and heard the cheer of his seamen as they saw the sails and rigging trailing over the side.

The Frenchman was now drifting helplessly before the gale.

It was only a question of a few more minutes before the battle was over.

Boats were lowered to pick up survivors but when Conrad was about to send a boarding party there was a sudden cry which he had expected.

'Fire! Fire!'

Flames leapt up from the sides of the French ship and ran along her decks.

Old ships because their timbers were dry, burnt quickly, and in a few minutes the whole vessel was ablaze.

Conrad could see men throwing themselves into the sea and he knew there were many more trapped below decks for whom there would be no escape.

When the survivors were brought aboard there were pitifully few of them and no officers.

He learnt that the ship was returning to France after being away for three years.

There was no doubt she had been responsible for the loss of a great many small British craft, and she had filled her holds with cargo the weight of which had made her effort to escape more difficult.

The prisoners were sent below and Conrad now enquired as to his own losses.

'One of a gun-crew killed, Sir,' Deakin informed him, 'not through enemy action but from the explosion of his own gun.'

Conrad's lips tightened, but he said nothing. This was a hazard all ships encountered sooner or later especially when the guns were new.

'Another man had his arm broken by the recoil of his gun, and two others were wounded by splinters when a shot scraped the upper deck.'

'Did it do any damage?' Conrad enquired.

'Little, Sir, that can't be repaired and re-painted.'

'Thank you, Commander.'

It was only then that Conrad remembered Delora and wondered if she had been afraid.

He was about to send Deakin to enquire, then thought he had best go himself.

By now, it was growing dusk and the wind had turned to rain.

Leaving Deakin in charge of clearing up the decks Conrad went below where the six cabins, of which he occupied one, were safer than what was normally the Captain's cabin on the quarter-deck.

Going to the cabin where he knew Delora would be, he met Abigail coming towards the companionway.

'Is it all over, Sir?' she asked in what he thought was an admirably calm voice.

'Yes, Abigail,' he replied. 'Is your mistress safe?'

'She'd like to see you, Sir. I was just about to make her a cup of tea.'

Conrad smiled feeling sure that like most English servants Abigail thought a cup of tea was a panacea for all ills.

'I am sure a cup of tea is what we all need,' he said.

He knew that what the men were expecting was a tot of rum all round and was sure it was something that Deakin would not overlook.

He opened the door of his cabin and as he did so, saw that as the lantern had not been lit, it was in semi-darkness.

For a moment there was silence and he thought perhaps Delora was not there. Then even as the thought flashed through his mind there was a little cry and she flung herself against him.

'You are .. safe! You have not been .. hurt?'

The words seemed to burst from her lips, and as the ship suddenly lurched he instinctively put his arms around her to hold her steady.

It was then as he felt the trembling of her slight body against him he was aware that her frightened little voice had died away and her face was turned up to his.

Without conscious volition, without thought, but obeying an impulse stronger than will, his lips found hers.

He knew as he touched her mouth that it was exactly as he had thought it would be in his dreams, soft, sweet, innocent and a wonder he had never known in his life before.

Because he was no longer himself but a stranger over whom he had no control, his arms tightened and he felt her quiver with an unmistakable rapture that matched his own.

He kissed her possessively, demandingly, and at the same time reverently because she was different in a way which for the moment he could not explain even to himself.

Only when the movement of the ship forced him to raise his head did Conrad come back to sanity.

'Forgive me,' he said almost inaudibly.

He was horrified at what he had done but for the moment he was not certain what he should do about it.

'I .. love you.'

The words were hardly above a whisper but he heard them.

'I know .. now that I have loved you from the first .. moment I saw you when I knew you were .. the man I had .. prayed would come to help me .. to save me!'

With a superhuman effort Conrad took his arms from Delora leaving her to hold onto the nearest chair which was battened down to the deck.

He walked away from her across the cabin to stand at the port-hole looking out into the gathering darkness outside, as if there he could find an answer to the pounding of his heart and the questions which already besieged his mind.

He did not speak, but he knew Delora moved with difficulty to an arm-chair and sat down.

Her head was turned towards him and although it was too dark to see clearly he knew, that her eyes seeking his face would be wise and questioning.

At last Conrad found his voice.

'You must forget what happened just now, Delora!' he said. 'It was something which would never have occurred except, I suppose, I was elated by our victory.'

There was silence, then Delora asked in a very small voice:

'A . are you .. saying that you are .. sorry you kissed me?'

'It is something which should not have happened.'

'But it .. did happen .. and I know now

that I .. love you.'

'That is something you should not say.'

'But it is .. true.'

'If it is, then it is extremely regrettable and you must do your best to convince yourself that it is only an illusion – something which is due to the fact that you are having an unusual experience in the middle of war, and that strange things do often occur at such times which are best forgotten.'

Again there was silence until Delora said, and now there was no mistaking there was a little sob in her voice:

'So .. you do not like .. kissing m . me! To me it was the most .. wonderful thing that ever happened!'

He realised she was perilously near to tears and he said quickly:

'Of course I liked kissing you, but I am ashamed of my lack of control. It is something of which any Captain would be ashamed.'

'I do not think you .. kissed me as a .. Captain,' Delora said, 'but as .. a man.'

This was so palpably true that Conrad had no answer.

As if he was afraid of what might be said next, he turned to the door remarking:

'I have a lot to do.'

'No .. please .. there is .. something I must .. say to you.'

Because he could not ignore her appeal, he moved towards her and sat down in a chair near to hers.

She put out her hands towards him and he took them because it would have been unkind to refuse to do so.

He felt her fingers tremble as he held them, but he forced himself not to kiss the softness of her skin as he longed to do.

He felt her hold onto him as if he was a lifeline that she could not relinquish. Then she said softly in a different voice than she had used before:

'I love you .. and even if you do not love me .. I shall go on loving you .. all my life .. until I .. die.'

'Delora, you must not say such things.'

'But they are true .. and because I love you .. I will do anything you .. want .. but please .. go on .. liking me even though I am your .. relation.'

'*Liking* you…!'

The two words burst from Conrad's lips. Then as he too was afraid of what he should say next, Delora bent forward in her chair and held his hands against her breast.

'I think,' she said in a whisper, 'that even .. though you are .. fighting against it, you do .. love me a .. little.'

Because they were practically in darkness and because the softness, the sweetness of her voice seemed almost to mesmerise him, while the nearness and the touch of her made his heart beat painfully, Conrad could no longer resist her.

'I love you! Of course I love you!' he said harshly. 'But you know as well as I do this is something which should never have happened.'

'But it *has* happened,' she said, 'and, oh .. my wonderful cousin, it is what I have .. prayed for.'

'But, my sweet, there is nothing we can do about our love,' Conrad protested. 'I am bound to carry out my orders and deliver you safely to the Governor and your brother in Antigua. That I have fallen in love with someone who is in my charge is against my own code of honour, apart from anyone else's.'

'When I was so terribly .. afraid that you might be .. killed or .. wounded in battle,' Delora answered, 'I knew that if you .. died I would .. want to .. die too.'

'You are not to talk like that,' Conrad said automatically.

As he spoke he was not quite certain how it happened, but she had moved from her chair into his and was in his arms, and he was kissing her as he had before, only more insistently.

He kissed her until he forgot everything but the magic of her lips, the softness and fragrance of her, and the wildness of his own love.

He could no longer think clearly, he only knew that Delora was everything that was his ideal.

There had always been a secret shrine in his heart in which was hidden the woman he wanted as his own, but whom he had thought never to find.

Now, as in the last few days he had learned

of the quickness of her mind, the beauty of her character, and the strength of her personality, it was all a part of his love.

Besides which, she was so utterly desirable and it was difficult not to believe that he had ever wanted any other woman.

He took his lips from Delora's and she whispered:

'Tell me that you love me .. tell me just once .. and I promise I will not bother you again.'

'Do you really think it is a bother?' Conrad asked. 'I love you, my precious little Delora, more than I can put into words, and much more than I can dare to contemplate.'

His hand touched her cheek as he said:

'I think you are a dream and not real, a dream of perfection that draws a man like a star which is always out of reach.'

As he knew she was going to say she was not out of reach but close beside him, it seemed superfluous to put it into words and Conrad was kissing her again.

It may have been a few minutes or a few centuries later they heard Abigail's voice outside and moved apart.

Conrad rose to his feet and was opening the lantern as Abigail came in followed by a steward carrying the tray on which were the tea-things.

As if she could not trust him she carried the tea-pot in her hands and quickly, for fear the movement of the ship might cause her to stumble, set it down on the table.

'Still in the dark, M'Lady?' she asked sharply.

'I am having trouble with this lantern,' Conrad replied as if she had spoken to him. 'See what you can do with it, Briggs.'

'Aye, aye, Sir!'

The steward set the tray down on the table.

'When you have had your tea, Cousin Delora,' Conrad said in a commendably ordinary voice, 'you will be able to return to your own cabin.'

He left as he spoke and wondered as he did so, if things would ever be the same as they had been when he went, after the battle, to look for Delora.

Fortunately for his peace of mind there was still a great deal of work waiting for him and a number of officers who wished to see him on one pretext or another.

Although he longed to do so, he did not see Delora again that evening and in consequence found it hard to sleep, thinking perhaps she was lonely without him.

'What am I to do now?' he asked himself in the darkness of his cabin as the *Invincible* sailed on through the night, creaking and groaning as if she too was in pain.

As he faced a new dawn he decided he must take a tight hold on himself and the kindest thing he could do, where Delora was concerned, was to convince her she was not really in love with him and what she felt was nothing but a school-girl's infatuation.

'After all, she has known very few men in her life,' he told himself. 'How can she be sure that this is the love that is real and lasting which at the moment she believes it to be?'

Then he told himself he would be be-littling something that was so beautiful, so unearthly, that to spoil anything so perfect would be committing a vandalism of which he should be deeply ashamed.

But that only brought him back to his original question.

What could he do?

He was still asking himself the same thing when he went up on the Poop deck, vividly conscious that Delora, in the cabin immediately below him, was lying in the big bed with its curved oak posts and blue curtains in which, when she disembarked at Antigua, he would sleep alone.

He knew when he did so, he would be haunted, as he would be at all other times in his life because in the space of only a few days she had entwined herself around his heart, so that he would never be free again.

Then he asked if it was really only an acquaintance of ten days that had made him feel as he did now.

He was certain in his own mind that fate had meant them for each other and perhaps they had known love together in other centuries. When he had seen her first standing in his cabin, although he had been afraid to admit it, perhaps they had recognised each other across eternity.

Deep in his thoughts he was suddenly

aware that a midshipman stood at his elbow.

'What is it, Campbell?'

'If you please, Sir, Lady Delora wishes to speak to you immediately.'

Conrad frowned.

He knew it would cause comment in the ship that Delora was sending for him so early in the morning and he decided he must warn her against such impulsive actions.

'Inform Her Ladyship,' he said to the midshipman, 'that I will be with her at the first available opportunity.'

'Aye, aye, Sir!'

The boy hurried away and Conrad deliberately had a long conversation with the man at the helm and the boatswain, before finally going down to the cabin where he knew Delora was waiting for him.

He knocked and when he heard her voice telling him to come in he entered, with what he hoped, was a slightly stern expression on his face.

He was, however, conscious that his heart was beating a little faster at the knowledge that he would see her and there was a throbbing in his temples which had been there, he thought, ever since he had kissed her.

Then when he saw the expression on her face he knew the reason she had sent for him was no ordinary one.

'What is the matter?'

For a moment it was hard for her to speak. Then she said:

'M . Mrs Melhuish .. died last n . night! Abigail found her a little .. while ago .. when she went to call her.'

'She is dead? How is it possible?' Conrad asked.

'She always said she had a .. weak heart,' Delora replied, 'but .. I am afraid because she had so many aches and p . pains I never believed her. Now I feel guilty that I did not .. sit with her when the battle was taking place.'

'You did what I ordered you to do.'

'Yes, I know,' Delora agreed, 'but I did ask Abigail what we should do about Mrs Melhuish and she replied that it would be an unkindness to move her when she was feeling so unwell.'

'I am sure Abigail was right,' Conrad said consolingly. 'Wait here. I will go and see what is happening.'

He went from the cabin to the one occupied by Mrs Melhuish.

It was very small and it had been intended for Barnet, but it was more comfortable than the accommodation a Captain's steward would expect in an older ship.

As he entered he found Abigail had already laid out the elderly lady, and with her eyes closed and her hands crossed on her breast she looked at peace.

'I am sorry about this, Abigail,' Conrad said.

'It can't be helped, Sir,' Abigail replied. 'She was a lady who was always ailing.'

'This means that Her Ladyship will be alone,' Conrad said, as if he was following his own thoughts.

'No more than she was while Mrs Melhuish was ill, and anyway she was no companion for a young girl.'

'But Her Ladyship should be chaperoned,' Conrad insisted.

'It's no use fretting, Sir,' Abigail said in the

tone of a Nanny speaking to a rather recalcitrant child. 'What's happened has happened, and nothing can undo it. Her Ladyship will be all right with people to talk to. That's what she's been missing living with only a lot of old servants and no companion of her own age.'

'But surely there must have been other young people in the neighbourhood?' Conrad asked.

'The neighbours who were the right type of people to be friends with Her Ladyship didn't approve of His Lordship.'

The way Abigail spoke told Conrad all too clearly what she herself thought of the Earl and, as if he knew nothing could be gained by furthering this conversation he said:

'I will instruct the ship's carpenter to make a coffin for Mrs Melhuish. I feel the sooner she is buried the better for Her Ladyship. There is no use in dwelling on these tragedies.'

'No, indeed, Sir,' Abigail agreed, 'and it would be a real kindness if Her Ladyship's not left alone too long with her thoughts.'

Conrad did not reply but he knew as he

walked away that it would be impossible to see only a little of Delora as he had half-intended to do.

Nothing could make her more miserable than she was already and the mere fact that Delora had spoken out so frankly made him aware that she too was afraid and apprehensive of the future.

'This is a hell of a mess!' he muttered to himself.

Then as the morning progressed and he went through his duties smoothly like a well-oiled machine, he knew that his mind, like his heart, was with the small, frightened girl alone in the Captain's cabin.

Mrs Melhuish was buried at sea that evening.

A small contingent of the Marines stood to attention while Conrad read the Burial Service because there was no Chaplain aboard.

There should have been one, but on the day they sailed Conrad was told that the Chaplain who had been posted to the *Invincible* was too ill to join them and there had been no time before they sailed to find a replacement.

Actually Conrad had been rather pleased.

His experience in the past of ship's Chaplains had not always been pleasant. Far too often they were men who could not make a success of their calling on shore and who for want of being offered a Parish chose to go to sea.

It was very rare to find one who could help and encourage the cabin-boys and midshipmen to get over their home-sickness, or to comfort men who were desperately unhappy at leaving their wives and families.

In fact a number of Chaplains were only too happy to sit drinking the voyage away or else wanting to deliver long, depressing sermons on Sundays until their time was strictly limited on Captain's orders.

Delora thought that Conrad read the Service more movingly than any Chaplain could have done.

She felt tears come into her eyes not only because she was sorry at Mrs Melhuish's death, but because she loved Conrad so overwhelmingly that even to look at him and hear his voice made her feel emotional.

'I love you!' she said in her heart as he said the last prayer.

Then she was praying, praying desperately that she need not leave him but be with him always.

'Please, God, please .. let us be together. Let me love him .. let me look after him .. and keep him safe.'

She felt as if her prayers winged out over the rolling sea and up into the grey sky, and because it was so intense she felt almost as if a cloud would open and a shaft of sunlight would tell her that God had heard her prayer.

But instead there was only the grey clouds, the indefinite horizon and the emptiness of the sea.

As the coffin went over the side and into the water the Marines presented arms while Conrad and the other officers saluted.

Now it was over and Mrs Melhuish was no longer with them.

Delora felt the tears blind her eyes, then Conrad was beside her leading her back to her cabin.

They went inside and he shut the door.

'It was very upsetting for you, Delora,' he said quietly.

'I am not really crying for her,' Delora replied, with a handkerchief to her eyes, 'but because .. death seems so .. final. If she had lived there might have been many more things .. for her to .. do and .. see.'

'That is something we feel when we are young,' Conrad said. 'But to the old there is peace and rest, and perhaps they ask nothing more.'

Delora gave him a sad little smile and took off her cape.

'You have an answer for everything,' she said. 'You are .. so wise.'

Her eyes met his, then she added very softly:

'And so .. marvellous!'

'If you say such things to me,' Conrad said, 'all my good resolutions as to our future behaviour will fly away. You have to help me to behave in the way I should – but it will not be easy.'

'And who will be impressed?' Delora asked. 'The sea, the stars, or my future husband who is marrying me for my money?'

The last words were spoken with such bitterness that Conrad was startled.

Then as if he could not help it he moved towards her and put his arms around her.

'Whatever happens,' he said, 'you are not to let it spoil you and you will face it with courage. But now, now at this moment, and until the voyage ends you must be happy, and I never wish to hear you speak in that tone again.'

Then he drew her closer and she hid her face against his shoulder, and when he had finished speaking, she did not move.

Then she looked up at him and he saw that the bitterness had gone from her eyes. Instead, and he knew it was because she was in his arms, there was a light that shone as if it came from her heart.

'Is that an order, Captain?' she enquired, and her lips were smiling.

CHAPTER FIVE

To Delora the days seemed to fly by on wings and everything was touched with the magic of sunlight even though the skies were dull and grey.

But soon the conditions changed so dramatically that it seemed as if one day they were labouring over leaden seas into a south-westerly gale with waves running as high as the yard arms, and the next there were blue skies and gentle breezes from the south-east.

The sea was blue, as blue as Delora's eyes, and there were flying fish and porpoises performing their antics with the grace of ballerinas.

It was all an enchantment that rested on the fact that Conrad was there and Delora could see him, hear his voice and, when they were alone, touch him.

Her love for him was like a light that

glowed within her and made her a hundred times more lovely than she had been before.

It was as if her happiness and his infected the whole ship.

The men sang and whistled as they worked and in the evenings there was the sound of the hornpipe coming from the lower decks.

Delora had not asked again that the men should play for her for the simple reason that Conrad had said there were no musical geniuses aboard, but their voices ringing out as they climbed the masthead or scrubbed down the decks were somehow very up-lifting.

Conrad seemed to relax in the happiness of the atmosphere: he gave dinner-parties in his cabin and when his officers were not entertaining Delora, he dined with her alone.

Sometimes his conscience pricked him, but as she had said: who was there to be impressed or scandalised by their be-haviour? All too soon they would reach Antigua, then he had sworn to himself that he would never see her again.

He knew he could not bear to know that she bore another man's name and, more unbearable, that she should be married to Grammell and that he and her despicable brother were rubbing their hands together with the anticipation of handling her fortune.

When he thought of it the agony was so intense that he would rise in the middle of the night to walk up and down the deck, knowing that only by exercising his body would he somehow be able to control the torment of his soul.

When he was alone with Delora it was a joy and a wonder which he told himself he would remember until he died.

'Tell me about yourself,' she would ask in her soft voice, 'what were you like when you were a little boy? And when did you first know that you wanted to go to sea?'

Conrad responded by telling her things he had never told any other woman, and the picture he drew for her of his childhood and his growing up made her not only love him the more, but know that she wanted to have a son who would be like him.

It was impossible to suppress the thought that if she did have a child by the man who was waiting to marry her, it might be as horrifying as he was, and she felt herself shiver at the idea.

Because they both loved each other too much to inflict unnecessary suffering, they tactfully did not speak of what would happen when they reached Antigua.

It was, nevertheless there in their minds and it was in the darkness of their eyes, and when Conrad saw Delora shiver and her lids droop pathetically, he would pull her into his arms and kiss her until she could think of nothing and nobody but him.

'Perhaps I have made a mistake,' she said one night.

Dinner was finished and they were sitting on the sofa, their hands linked together.

'What sort of mistake?' he asked.

'Perhaps .. because the world is round .. we shall go on travelling without sighting land .. and sail and sail into infinite space.'

Conrad laughed.

'We must find land soon. Our stores are becoming depleted and we need vegetables, fruit and most of all fresh water.'

'Abigail insists on boiling everything I drink.'

'That is very wise of her,' Conrad commended, 'but even so, I shall be glad when we can refill the water-butts, and when you see fruit growing on the trees and a profusion of flowers everywhere you look, you will know that you are in the West Indies.'

There was silence and he knew what else was waiting for them in the West Indies and so he took Delora in his arms.

Then they could only whisper of themselves, and everything else was of no importance.

Each day grew warmer and Delora no longer walked about in her fur-lined cloak but appeared in attractive muslin gowns and soon needed a sunshade to protect herself from the heat of the sun.

It was a day when everything seemed to be golden, and Conrad on the Poop deck was avidly aware of Delora on the deck below him, so lovely in her summer attire that she might have been dressed for a garden-party.

He could not help looking at her and as if

the magnetism of his eyes drew hers, she looked up at him with a smile that illuminated her small face.

For a moment they were as close as if they were in each other's arms and Conrad could almost feel her heart beating in unison with his.

Then, like a voice from another sphere he heard the look-out call:

'Sails ho! And Oi thinks Oi heard gunfire!'

Conrad sent a midshipman up the mast head and a few minutes later he called:

'I think there are several ships ahead, Sir, but I can't be sure.'

Deakin appeared at Conrad's side to ask:

'Shall I clear for action, Sir?'

'Yes, Commander,' Conrad replied, 'and have the guns loaded and run out too, if you please.'

There was enough wind to keep the *Invincible* steady on her course and a short while later Conrad could see through a glass what was happening.

There was a small convoy of four or five merchantmen all flying the British flag and attacking them were two Privateers.

They were, without exception, the largest and finest ships of their type Conrad had ever seen at sea, and he was certain they were newly built, strongly armed and the merchantmen had no chance against them.

As they drew nearer he could see that the British ships were huddled together, each ship closer to its neighbour than any merchant captain could be induced to steer unless activated by fear.

Boarding nettings had been set up on their decks and they were running out their guns.

But Conrad knew any defence they could offer would be feeble, though the fact that they could defend themselves at all was a help.

He knew long before they were within range what his problem would be. It was that if the *Invincible* opened fire on the Privateers it would be impossible not to damage the merchant ships at the same time.

As if the Privateers were well aware of this they were working to windward so as to have the merchantmen between them and the *Invincible*.

With their sharp, black hulls and steeply raked masts they were, even though they were the enemy, a beautiful sight which any seaman would be forced to admire.

There would be at least one hundred and fifty men aboard each ship and with the wind on their quarters, the white water foaming at their bows, lying over in the breeze, they were a picture of malignant efficiency.

Conrad knew that to attack them as he wanted to do, he had somehow to get between them and the convoy. Then as if they were aware of his intention they changed course zooming in on the nearest merchantman and he saw the flash of their guns.

Conrad was astute enough to realise it would not be their intention to sink the merchantmen. What they wanted was their cargo, and if possible, the ships themselves to send to the nearest American Port as a prize capture.

He was quite certain the superior guns of the Privateers and the manner in which they were intimidating the convoy would have a bad effect on the morale of the crews of the merchant ships.

He stared at the enemy, calculating their speed, observing their course.

The Privateer to starboard would arrive at the convoy first and he would have a minute or two in hand to deal with the second Privateer if he disposed of this one.

'Starboard and two points!' he called.

'Starboard and two points!' echoed the Quarter-master.

The *Invincible* swung round and managing to hold the wind swept between the Privateer and the nearest merchantman.

There was very little space to spare, but the *Invincible* managed it, and the Captain of the merchantman keeping his head, moved his ship as swiftly as he could out of the way.

'Stand to your guns!' Conrad bellowed. 'Commander, give the Privateer a broadside as we pass her!'

There was the resounding explosion of the guns which appeared all to fire at the same moment.

Then as Conrad saw the Privateer's masts

falling and felt a cheer rise in his throat, a red hot coal from Hell struck him in the leg and the world disintegrated into a sudden darkness.

Conrad came back to consciousness to hear voices raised and he wondered why they should make so much damned noise when his head felt as if it was splitting open and something heavy appeared to be holding him down on a hard surface.

Then through a mist which gradually evolved from black into crimson, he heard a voice he recognised, saying:

'I must insist, My Lady, on doing my duty. I'm the Surgeon, and it's my decision whether I do or do not amputate!'

'I will not allow you, whatever you may say, to remove Captain Horn's leg without his permission!'

The voice was soft but firm, and as Conrad realised who was speaking he opened his eyes:

He tried to ask what the devil was going on, but for the moment the words would not come to his lips.

Then as he saw a number of heads and shoulders above him he realised that he was lying on the amputation table on the upper deck and with a sudden tug of his heart, he wondered where he had been wounded.

Now he could see Delora bending over him and he heard her say:

'You are awake! Can you hear me?'

'I – can – hear – you.'

His voice started weak, but grew a little stronger.

'Listen, Cousin Conrad, this is important,' Delora said. 'The Surgeon wishes to amputate your leg. But you have only been hit by grape-shot, and I know that Abigail and I can treat it so that you will be able to walk again.'

'That's extremely unlikely, Captain,' the Surgeon intervened, 'and if gangrene sets in, you know as well as I do, Sir, that you'll die!'

'Please, Conrad, please let us try to save it,' Delora pleaded.

It seemed to Conrad that it was his head which was wounded and everything seemed far away so that it was difficult to concentrate.

Then as he forced himself to do so, he knew that Delora was speaking sense. He had always loathed the ship's Surgeons who chopped the men up as if they were nothing but ox-meat.

'I am – in your – hands,' he said to Delora.

His voice was weak and as if the effort of speaking had been too much for him, he closed his eyes, but he heard her give a little cry as she said to the Surgeon on the other side of the table:

'You have your orders. I will nurse Captain Horn, and you can see to anyone else who needs your attention.'

'Your Ladyship'll live to rue this day!' the Surgeon replied disagreeably.

He walked away but he left his instruments behind and as Abigail picked up a probe Delora said:

'Have you the laudanum with you?'

'It's here, M'Lady.'

'Then I will give it to him if he regains consciousness, but in the meantime see if you can remove the grape-shot.'

It was a long time afterwards that Conrad

was to learn that fortunately it was a shot from one of the smaller guns on the Privateer that had hit him.

The force of the shot had thrown him to the deck, and as it did so, he hit his head against the navigating instruments which had rendered him unconscious.

He had been carried down to the amputation table on the orlop deck and while the Surgeon was attending to another wounded man, Barnet had run to tell Delora what had happened.

It was a strict and inviolable rule that the wounded should take their turn, the first brought down was the first to be dressed. No favour was shown to any man, be he officer or swabber.

The fact that Conrad had to wait saved him from having his leg chopped off the moment the Surgeon sighted him.

By the time Delora and Abigail arrived Barnet had cut away Conrad's white breeches and they could see the mess which had been made by the grape-shot.

They were, however, obviously only flesh wounds in his thigh, and though unpleasantly deep, the bone was intact and unbroken.

The wounds were also all above the knee which apparently was not injured, and Abigail said at once that if they could get the grape-shot out and prevent it from festering there was every chance they could save the whole leg.

Delora was well aware of how Conrad would feel if he was crippled.

She had seen many legless men in the last few years, men who had been wounded at sea or in the Army, hobbling about with wooden stumps or struggling on crutches.

'We must save his leg .. we must, Abigail!' she cried.

'I think it's possible, M'Lady,' Abigail replied in her slow, calm voice, 'but it'll mean probing deep and hurting him a great deal.'

Delora had remembered that when Lord Nelson's arm had been amputated the only thing he had been given to help him after the operation had been performed, was opium.

She knew that Mrs Melhuish frequently

took small doses of laudanum to relieve the pain of an aching head, and she sent Barnet running to the dead woman's cabin to see if it was still there.

He returned with a bottle which was three-quarters full and as Abigail took it from him, she thought that at least Conrad would not have to suffer the agonies of men who were given nothing more than a tot of rum or a leather pad on which to bite during the operation.

It was at that moment that the Surgeon, having finished with his first patient came to the amputation table.

He was rubbing a knife with a blood-stained rag, saying as he did so:

'Your Ladyship had best return to your cabin. This is not the sort of sight you'd wish to see.'

It was then that the argument started and when the Surgeon walked away in a temper, Abigail began to probe in the torn and bleeding flesh.

It was not a pretty sight, but Delora watched Conrad's face and when he began to show signs of consciousness she made him swallow several spoonfuls of laudanum and he slipped away into a dark slumber.

It was not until the middle of the night that Conrad opened his eyes again and for a moment he could not think where he was or what had happened.

He was certainly in a strange bed, and by the light of the lantern he could see it had carved oak posts.

Then he knew there was somebody beside him and found it was Abigail.

She put a hand on his forehead, found it was hot and wet with sweat, and lifting his head so that he could drink, put something sweet and cool to his lips.

As his head rested again on the pillow, he remembered the argument on the upper deck and asked:

'My – leg?'

'You still have it,' Abigail replied, 'so go to sleep, Sir. That's what you need – sleep!'

He thought later there must have been something in the drink she had given him, for he fell asleep immediately.

When next he awoke, the cabin was bright

with sunshine and it haloed Delora's head with gold as he looked up into her face.

'Can you hear me, Conrad?' she asked.

He tried to smile at her and was conscious as he did so, that he felt very hot and there was something heavy on his forehead.

She took it away and replaced it with a cloth that was cool and moist.

His whole body seemed to be burning, and he knew that he had a fever and hoped as Delora was beside him, it was not infectious. Then he drifted away again into a grey 'No-man's-land' where he need no longer think or wonder why he was so hot.

It was a few days before he could think clearly and the first thing he realised was that he was in the Captain's cabin which he had given up to Delora.

'Why am I here?' he demanded.

'Her Ladyship insisted, Sir,' Abigail replied, 'and it's more convenient for us to nurse you here than if you were on the deck below.'

'Where is Her Ladyship sleeping?' Conrad demanded.

'In Mrs Melhuish's cabin, and she's comfortable enough. There's no need to be worrying yourself about anything except getting well and proving to that butcher who calls himself a Surgeon that we were right and he was wrong!'

Conrad wanted to laugh at the asperity in Abigail's voice.

In the days that followed his leg was so painful, especially when it was being dressed, that he sometimes thought it would have been best if he had lost it.

But that was only a passing thought when the pain was almost unbearable.

He refused to take any more laudanum, even when Abigail cleaned the wound with spirit which was brandy.

He was aware that this was saving him from gangrene, and he was interested to see that Abigail's dressings, which she changed twice daily, were applied with honey.

'As soon as we reach land I'll find some herbs which will cure you more quickly than anything that Surgeon can suggest,' she said in her tart manner.

Conrad tried to smile but he was concentrating his whole will-power in a determined effort to justify Delora's faith that he would walk again without any support.

As soon as his head was free of the mists caused both by his fall and the laudanum, he had sent for the First Lieutenant to find out what had happened.

'We sank the first Privateer,' Deakin said gleefully, 'and the second with Watkinson in command, is on its way to Plymouth.'

'A prize the Admiralty will undoubtedly welcome!' Conrad exclaimed, 'because there is no doubt that the American ship-builders can teach us quite a lot we do not know about fast ships.'

'I have never seen a better designed craft for the work for which it was required,' Deakin replied, 'and as the Navy will pay for it, that'll mean a nice sum in your pocket, Sir.'

'And in yours, Deakin,' Conrad replied.

They both grinned knowing that prize-money was divided in proportion amongst the Captain and the crew of the vessel that captured her.

'How many casualties?'

'Two men killed outright, Brown and Higgins, and twelve wounded.'

Conrad frowned but Deakin quickly spoke of something else.

It was then Conrad asked the question which had been hovering in the forefront of his mind during the night.

'How many days before we reach Antigua?'

'Another nine or ten,' the First Lieutenant replied. 'I'm trying to keep her on a steady keel, Sir, since you've been ill, and it's always wise to go slower when a ship has a certain amount of damage.'

'Damage?' Conrad questioned sharply.

'It's nothing very serious, but it'll undoubtedly take several weeks in a dock-yard before we're fit to fight another battle.'

Conrad was not certain whether he was glad or sorry that he would have to stay in Antigua.

He had made up his mind that the moment he had set Delora ashore and replenished his stores he would put as many miles between himself and her as was possible.

He knew he could not endure the misery of seeing her with a man whose real interest lay in her fortune.

Delora must have asked the same question as he had for after Deakin had gone, she had come and sat on the side of his bed and slipped her hand into his.

'We still have more than a week together,' she said softly.

'I suppose I should thank you for keeping me alive and a whole man,' Conrad answered, 'but at the moment I am asking myself if I would not be better dead.'

'While there is .. life there is .. hope,' Delora said softly, 'and because I believe not only in prayer .. but that God is merciful .. I still have .. hope.'

Conrad drew in his breath.

'My precious, has there ever been anyone as perfect as you?'

'Or as brave and wonderful as you?' she replied.

She told him how first the officers, then almost every member of the crew, had come the first night after the battle to the cabin to ask how he was and reassure themselves that he was still alive.

'So many of them said they could not lose you because there had never been a Captain like you.'

There was a pause before Delora went on:

'It was not only because they admire you for your bravery and your victories, but because you are kind and treat them as men rather than animals.'

She knew her words pleased Conrad and because he wanted to hear about his men, she told him little bits of gossip to keep him amused.

'If only we had better food to give him!' Abigail grumbled, as she stewed the salted beef until it could be made into a broth, and ransacked the ship's stores for anything she thought would give Conrad more strength.

She refused to allow him to be bled as was usual, when he had a fever, and the Surgeon had gone about muttering that the Captain's days were numbered.

One man had died while his arm was being amputated and another who had his foot removed because of a splinter which had inserted itself under the skin during the

161

engagement, had died after three days of agony.

Delora refused to tell Conrad about it and warned both Deakin and Barnet not to do so.

'It will only upset him,' she said, 'and he will feel guilty that we saved his leg while we were unable to stop the Surgeon from doing his worst on those other wretched men.'

'It is always taken for granted that a man who has been wounded must lose the limb that is injured, there being no other way of keeping him alive,' Commander Deakin said.

'There are other ways, as you see now,' Delora replied, 'and perhaps when Conrad returns to England he will be able to show himself to the Admiralty as an example of what can be done if only we had a little more knowledge.'

'I doubt if anyone in the Admiralty would listen,' Deakin said grimly. 'They hate new ideas and innovations. If we could find somebody to speak about it in Parliament, that would be a different thing.'

'I am sure Conrad would know somebody,' Delora said confidently.

She wondered as she spoke, whether there would be any use asking her brother to support such a contention in the House of Lords.

Then when she remembered Denzil's utter indifference to anything which did not concern his own comfort or amusement she knew what a foolish idea it was.

'In a few days I shall see him,' she thought.

The idea was so horrifying that the moment it was possible, she ran to the Captain's cabin, determined not to waste a minute of time when she might be with Conrad.

Abigail and Barnet had just finished dressing his leg and he was lying back against the pillows rather white-faced, his lips set in a hard line.

As Delora came towards him looking like spring itself he smiled at her and forgot his own sufferings.

'Did you sleep well?' she asked.

'I lay and thought about you,' he replied.

Barnet and Abigail had left the cabin, to dispose of the soiled dressings and to fetch

Conrad a cup of tea.

'It is going to be hot today,' Delora said. 'Shall we carry you up on deck so that you can be in the sunshine?'

Conrad considered for a moment, then he said:

'I think Abigail will insist that I rest as much as possible because when we dock I must go ashore.'

'Where .. will you .. stay?'

It was the first time they had discussed what they would do once they had arrived and he heard the fear in Delora's voice.

'I hope I shall be able to stay in Admiral Nelson's house which is by the edge of the dockyard.'

There was a little pause, then Delora asked in a very small voice:

'And how .. far away will .. I be?'

Conrad took both her hands in his.

'I do not know, my precious,' he said. 'Government House is at St John's, several miles away. But there is another house which stands on a hill just above the dock-yard.'

He saw Delora's eyes looking at him

intently, and he went on:

'It is called Clarence House, and it was built in 1787 for Prince William, Duke of Clarence. He lived in Antigua when he commanded the *Pegasus*.'

'You think I might stay there?'

'It is only an idea I had because somebody told me the Governor used it as a country house, and I think it unlikely that you will move into Government House until you are actually married.'

At the last word Delora gave a little cry and bent her head so that her forehead was resting against Conrad's hands as he covered hers.

'How .. can I .. bear it? How can I .. marry anyone but .. you?'

He could hardly hear the words as they tumbled from her lips and yet he knew only too well what she was saying.

His fingers tightened until hers were bloodless, and though he desperately wanted to comfort her, he knew there was nothing he could say, nothing he could do.

Then as they heard the door open and Abigail come back into the cabin, Delora sprang to her feet and walked to a port-hole so that she could hide her tears.

A week later they had their last dinner together by candlelight as they had dined the first evening when they had been alone.

The menu was a very different one, but it would not have mattered if they had been served ambrosia and nectar because they could think of nothing but themselves and their love.

Neither Conrad nor Delora would start to speak, then as their eyes met, the words would die away and they could only look at each other as heart spoke to heart and soul to soul.

'You will not .. forget me?' Delora asked later when the food had been taken away.

As soon as it had gone she sat beside Conrad on the bed on his uninjured side and he put his arm around her so that she could lay her head against his shoulder.

He kissed her forehead but not her lips, and she knew that for the moment both of them were trying not to be too emotional for fear that their feelings would sweep away the last vestiges of control.

'You know that would be impossible,' Conrad answered in a low voice. 'You know too that wherever I am, even if there is a whole world between us, I shall feel that you are with me, guiding me, helping me and loving me as you are now.'

'That is what .. I feel,' Delora said, 'but, darling, if only I could .. die I should be .. with you, then there would be no more problems.'

There was something in the way she spoke which made Conrad say sharply:

'You told me that while there is life there is hope. So let us both believe that one day fate will be kind and we shall be together in this world.'

She drew a little closer to him and he knew that she was thinking that Lord Grammell was an old man and perhaps they would not have to wait so very long.

But to Conrad it was an agony worse than anything he had endured from the wound in his leg, to wonder what would happen to Delora until Grammell died.

He had not been with her without

realising how innocent she was not only of the world but the ways of men. She had no idea of the depths of depravity to which men like Grammell and her brother could sink in their search for what they called 'pleasure'.

The thought of her being shocked and appalled by what she would learn at the hands of these creatures turned Conrad into a would-be murderer, and he thought he should be man enough to destroy them both before they could hurt anyone as sensitive and spiritual as Delora.

He knew there was nothing he could say which could prepare her for the ordeal which lay ahead, and like her he could only pray for a miracle, but what it could be, he had not the slightest idea.

Delora stayed with Conrad until he knew that he must be unselfish and force her to rest.

'You must go to bed, my lovely darling,' he said.

'Do you .. really want me to .. leave you?'

'You know I never want you to do that,' he replied. 'I want you with me always and for ever, but we have, both of us, to try and do what is right.'

She turned very gently so as not to hurt him, and put her arms around his neck.

'I love you with all my heart, because I cannot .. help it,' she said, 'but I also love you with my mind and soul because you are everything that is wise, noble and good. Whatever happens to me, I shall try to behave as you would .. wish me to do, so that you will be .. proud of me.'

She spoke so simply and sincerely that Conrad felt the tears prick his eyes.

He told himself it was because he was so weak from his wound, but he knew there was no other woman of his acquaintance, or perhaps in the world, who would behave so courageously at this particular moment.

He held her very close against him and when he kissed her it was not with the passion they had known so often before, but with a love that for the moment was not human, but wholly divine and sacred.

He felt her cling to him and knew that if he could die to save her he would do so.

At the same time he must live and

somehow give her the inner strength he had always had himself so that she would not kill herself.

He was aware the idea was vaguely at the back of her mind and because he was afraid that would happen, he said:

'Believe, my darling, and pray. Pray that one day we shall find happiness and a new life together.'

He felt her arms tighten around his neck and he went on:

'The darkest hour is always before the dawn, and that is what we are going through now. I have a feeling that we both know the dawn will come. Promise me that you will not allow yourself to despair but will go on believing.'

'I believe .. in you,' Delora answered. 'Will you swear to me on everything you hold sacred that you believe we have a chance, a real chance of being together one day?'

Conrad was still for a moment, then he said:

'Sometimes when I have been in a battle in which all the odds have been stacked against me, when it seemed impossible for me not to be defeated and perhaps an-nihilated, I have known in a strange way that I cannot explain, that I shall be victorious.'

'And .. you feel that now? You really .. feel it?' Delora enquired.

'I swear to you not only on all I hold sacred, but on you, who are more holy to me than anything else in Heaven or earth, that I know in my heart and in my mind that one day we will be together.'

Delora gave a little cry.

'Oh, Conrad, darling, I will believe that too, and we will both pray that it may be soon!'

'Pray God let it be soon, very soon!' Conrad said quietly before he kissed her again.

CHAPTER SIX

There was very little wind and anyway Deakin did not press the *Invincible* during the night.

This was not only in consideration for his Captain's comfort, but also because he had not told Conrad how much damage had actually been done by the Privateers to the lower deck of the *Invincible*.

Damage to the lower decks of a ship was always dangerous because when she changed course or the sea was rough, it was easy to ship water.

They therefore sailed slowly through the smooth sea and in the morning Delora learned that they would dock about noon.

She went to see Conrad as soon as Abigail had finished dressing his wounds, and found him sitting up in bed while Barnet had already arranged what clothes he would wear on a chair.

She looked at them doubtfully and said:

'Are you wise to dress?'

'As far as I am able to do so,' Conrad replied, 'I intend to arrive in style.'

He smiled as he spoke, but Delora knew he was serious in that he intended to show her brother and Lord Grammell that he had some authority although whether it would be any use as far as she was concerned, they neither of them had any idea.

She walked towards the bed and he put his hand out towards her, saying as he did so:

'You look very beautiful this morning, my darling.'

She held onto him as if she was drowning in the despair of her own thoughts. Then she said:

'I have .. something to ask you.'

'What is it, my precious?'

'Will you be as .. nice as possible to Denzil and .. try not to let him see your .. real feelings for him?'

Conrad was surprised but questioned in a quiet voice:

'Why are you asking me to do this?'

'Because Abigail feels it is important that

she should go on dressing your wound, and I do not want Denzil to refuse to allow her to do so.'

'Do you think he might do that?'

Delora hesitated a moment before she said:

'You must know that he hates you!'

Conrad raised his eye-brows.

'I cannot conceive of any reason why he should do so, unless of course, you are referring to the family feud.'

'There is a much more personal reason than that.'

'I have no idea what it can be.'

'Have you forgotten that you are the heir presumptive to the title until Denzil has a son?'

If she had intended to startle Conrad, she had certainly succeeded.

For a moment he stared at her incredulously. Then he asked:

'Is that the truth?'

'But of course it is!' Delora replied. 'I thought you must be aware of it.'

'I had not the slightest idea!' Conrad said. 'To begin with, just as I did not know of your existence, I had no idea how many children your father had. He might have had six sons.'

'He had an only son and he was one himself,' Delora answered, 'and so far Denzil's wife, Charlotte, who is a pleasant woman, has only three daughters.'

She paused before she said in a low voice:

'She was very ill with the last one, and because Denzil was so angry with her because the baby was not a boy, the doctors insisted that she should have rest and quiet. That is one of the reasons why he came to Antigua.'

Everything Conrad had heard about his Cousin Denzil made him dislike him more than he already did, but for Delora's sake he did not say so.

As he did not speak after a moment she said:

'I want to be able to see you .. I must see you after we arrive .. so please .. Conrad, darling .. be nice to Denzil .. and we can only hope that he will make no objection to our meeting .. or to Abigail nursing you.'

Because she did not want to worry him,

she added quickly:

'Of course she has told Barnet exactly what to do if Denzil takes me away to another part of the island, but I am praying that we shall be in the house that you spoke of .. and .. near to .. you.'

Conrad was not sure if this would be a joy or an agony.

He could only wait, as he knew Delora was waiting, apprehensively for them to reach the dockyard where he anticipated that Denzil would greet them.

While he was being dressed, Delora went up on deck and had her first glimpse of the heavily wooded islands.

As they sailed through a sea more blue than she had imagined any sea could be, she could see the green bays which Conrad had told her were all around the island with their white and gold sand beaches.

Because she was interested he had informed her that the trees were red and white cedars and mahogany, while along the shore coconut palms and mangroves grew.

As they drew nearer to the land she could see, as she expected, the flaming blooms of the red poinsettias and patches of other brilliant flowers that she had read about.

Then she had her first sight of what the First Lieutenant told her was called the English harbour with Nelson's Dock-yard and a fine building just above it, which she was to learn later, was Clarence House.

Only when the *Invincible* was letting down her anchor did Delora feel suddenly afraid of the man who was waiting for her on the shore, and felt her lips were dry with the fear she had almost forgotten during her last weeks of happiness.

Then as the seamen hurried about taking in the sails, she saw a boat put out from the shore and knew who would be in it.

She turned to one of the officers standing near her.

'Will you tell the Captain, Mr Lloyd,' she asked, 'that I think the Earl of Scawthorn is approaching us?'

The Lieutenant sent a midshipman with the message and just as the boat reached the ship and a rope-ladder was let down, Conrad was brought on deck.

He was carried in a chair which Barnet

had made for him in which his legs were supported by a rest and covered with a rug.

He was wearing his uniform coat with his decorations, his China silk scarf was tied immaculately round his neck and his gold lace hat was on his dark head.

He looked almost well except that much of the tan had faded from his cheeks and his face was thinner from the amount of blood he had lost and also the pain he had endured.

Those who were close to him like Delora and Abigail were aware what a stupendous effort it had been to make himself ready to receive the man he loathed and despised.

Denzil was piped aboard, the Marines presented arms, the officers saluted, and Delora stepped forward to curtsy before Denzil kissed her cheek.

'So – you are here!'

There was something gloating, she thought, in the way he said the words, and she knew that his eyes with the deep lines of debauchery beneath them, were flicking over her taking in every detail of her appearance, as if she was a horse he was putting up for a sale.

With an effort she said:

'Yes I am here .. but it has been a somewhat .. adventurous voyage.'

'We had news yesterday that you had been in action,' the Earl answered.

'The Captain will tell you about it,' Delora said quickly. 'I do not know whether you are aware, Denzil, but he is our cousin, Conrad Horn.'

'So I have learned from an Admiralty communique which told me in which ship you were travelling.'

Delora knew from the note in his voice that he had not been pleased at the information.

He walked across the deck to where Conrad was waiting for him.

'So we meet after many years of animosity, Cousin,' Denzil said. 'And I see that you are somewhat the worse for wear.'

Delora drew in her breath at the jeering way in which he spoke, but Conrad put out his hand.

'Welcome aboard the *Invincible!* I can only regret I am not in the position to offer you

179

any extensive hospitality.'

'There is no necessity for that,' the Earl replied. 'You have brought me what you were asked to bring, and I imagined you would then be glad to return to the battle area off the coast of France.'

'Apparently our enemies are to be found not only in European waters.'

As Conrad spoke he saw there was an undoubted scowl on the Earl's forehead and there was a look in his eyes which instantly made him suspicious.

He had known that when Nelson was in Antigua he had found the Governor was far too lax in his treatment of the Americans who ever since, after the Declaration of Independence, were no longer entitled to the rights possessed by British citizens.

As Colonists they had enjoyed a very prosperous trade with the West Indies, and they could not see why now they should be debarred after they had become what was, to all intents and purposes, a foreign power.

Nelson had protested and acting as he saw fit, he had seized many of the American trading ships.

He had incurred so much displeasure that as he said himself: 'I was persecuted from one island to another, so that I could not leave my ship.'

Conrad had often thought that, when everybody applauded and recounted Nelson's physical courage, the moral courage he had displayed in the West Indies when he was in conflict with his Senior Officer showed him in a dazzling light unlit by cannon or thundering sails.

Nelson had won and the Governor having had his attention drawn to the Navigation Act, had finally been forced to take action.

Now Conrad was suspicious after what the First Lord had said that the new Privateers were ready to recompense in one way or another, a Governor who was prepared to turn a blind eye to their activities.

All this flashed through his mind, but he merely said blandly and disarmingly:

'I am afraid not only the *Invincible* needs some repairs but so do I.'

'Then of course you must take things easy until you are completely well again,' the Earl answered.

As he spoke Conrad thought he was pleased at the idea that if he was laid up he would certainly not be able to go snooping around, pushing his nose into places where he was not wanted.

'Cousin Conrad has been very ill indeed,' Delora said quickly, 'and I think we should find somewhere ashore where he can stay while the ship is being repaired.'

'Yes, of course,' Denzil agreed, as if he had just thought of it. 'I imagine he will find the Admiral's House which is empty at the moment, the best place to accommodate him.'

'I should be extremely grateful if that could be arranged,' Conrad said, as he knew he was expected to say.

'I know Lord Grammell, who is at present in St John's,' Denzil said, 'would wish me to make proper arrangements for you, and I will therefore take Delora ashore with me and inform them at the Admiral's House to expect you.'

'That is exceedingly kind of you,' Conrad replied, 'and will you both be travelling to St John's?'

He was aware as he spoke, that Delora drew in her breath.

'As it happens,' the Earl answered, 'the Governor has put Clarence House at my disposal, and I intend that my sister and I should stay there while we arrange her marriage.'

Without looking at Delora, Conrad was aware of the relief in her eyes, and now the Earl, as if he had nothing more to say to the cousin he disliked, remarked sharply to his sister:

'We had best be going ashore. Your luggage can follow.'

'Yes, of course,' Delora said, 'and would you wish that Abigail comes with us, or shall she follow later?'

'Abigail?' her brother repeated.

Then as if for the first time he was aware there should have been another woman aboard, he enquired:

'Where is Mrs Melhuish? I ordered her to come with you.'

'I have not had time to tell you, Denzil,' Delora replied, 'but Mrs Melhuish died during the first battle we had in the Atlantic.'

This was obviously something the Earl had not expected, and there was a momentary pause before he remarked:

'She always was a tiresome woman and I cannot imagine anything more inconvenient than for her to die at that particular moment.'

'She could not .. help it,' Delora murmured.

She was acutely conscious that the Lieutenants, as well as the Marines standing round them, were listening to their conversation, and she thought they would be shocked that her brother should speak in such an unfeeling manner about somebody who had died when she was merely doing her duty.

As if his mind was on something other than Mrs Melhuish's death, the Earl said almost as if he spoke to himself:

'I suppose as you had Abigail with you, you were properly looked after?'

He shot a suspicious glance at Conrad as he spoke, who knowing exactly what he was thinking, wished that he could knock him down.

How dare anyone even imagine that if Delora was alone on the ship he or any other man would have taken advantage of her position?

Then even as he felt his anger rise, he knew this was the sort of behaviour that might be expected of Denzil and he was not likely to give any other man credit for being decent and chivalrous.

As if in answer to the unpleasantness of the Earl's suspicions, Abigail appeared at that moment on deck.

In her black dress with her plain bonnet and her greying hair she looked, Conrad thought, the embodiment of respectability and propriety.

She walked towards Denzil and dropped him a small curtsy.

'Good-day, M'Lord.'

'I hope you have been looking after your mistress properly after the untimely death of Mrs Melhuish,' the Earl said sharply.

'Her Ladyship has been in my care, M'Lord, as she has been ever since she was born!' Abigail retorted.

It was an answer with which it was

impossible for the Earl to find fault, and he walked away to the side of the ship saying as he did so:

'Come along! There is no point in wasting time here when there is a great deal to do ashore.'

Delora ignored the urgency in his tone. She curtsied to Conrad and held out her hand.

'Thank you for all your kindness,' she said, 'and for the very happy time I have had in this magnificent ship which has proved herself worthy of her name.'

It was difficult to say the words she had rehearsed to herself before she left her cabin, and only as she finished did she raise her eyes to Conrad's and feel her heart turn over in her breast.

Then she shook hands with the First Lieutenant who had joined them on deck and all the Lieutenants.

Only when she had finished and heard her brother shout at her from the boat below, did she turn back to Mr Deakin to say:

'You will be very careful how you take him ashore? His wounds must not start bleeding again.'

'I promise you we will look after him,' he replied.

Then at another shout from the Earl she hurriedly climbed down into the boat and a moment later it was pulling away from the ship.

Clarence House was not a large building but a very attractive one, set on the hill which overlooked the dock-yard.

It was different from any house that Delora had ever been in before and the view over the green bays and sea was breath-taking.

She was concerned at the moment only with what plans her brother had for her, and he did not delay in telling her what they were.

'I have sent a message to the Governor to tell him of your arrival,' he said when she joined him in the comfortable Drawing-Room. 'He will undoubtedly arrive this evening to stay here. That is why I have given you the small bed-room for the present. You will share the largest one with him as soon as you are married.'

Delora felt the colour rise in her cheeks and her brother went on:

'I was not quite certain of the actual day of your arrival, but there is no point in delaying your wedding. The sooner we can send evidence of it to those damned Trustees in New York, the quicker they will be forced to hand over your money.'

'Why do you need it so badly?' Delora asked. 'I always thought Papa was a very rich man.'

'He was!' Denzil replied, 'but things have become much more expensive since the war.'

She knew as he spoke, that was not the real reason why he needed money, and she was sure that it was his wild extravagances that had brought him to the point where he must 'sell' his own sister to replenish his pockets.

But there was no point in saying so and making him disagreeable, so she merely said:

'As you know, Denzil, I have no wish to marry a man I have never seen. I think it would be wise if Lord Grammell and I got to know each other, before our marriage takes place.'

Denzil poured himself another drink from the decanter that was standing beside his chair.

'Grammell knows all about you he wishes to know,' he replied, 'and that is that you are rich! It is damned expensive being a Governor, even in an out-of-the-way hole like this, although I dare say you will enjoy the power it will give you, once you are his wife.'

'Lord Grammell may know all he wishes to know about me,' Delora said, 'but I know nothing about him, except that he is a very old man.'

'Are you making difficulties?' Denzil asked aggressively. 'Well, let me make this clear to you, Delora – you will marry who I tell you to marry and when I tell you to do so. If not, I will make things so unpleasant that you will rue the day you were ever born!'

He spoke so ferociously that without being aware of it, she took a step further away from him.

She had forgotten when she had been with Conrad, how frightening her brother could be, and she thought now, as he glared at her with his eyes too close together that there was something about him which made her feel that he was not quite sane.

'I suppose,' he went on, 'because you have been flaunting yourself about on a ship before all those men, you have got new ideas of getting your own way. Well, let me make this clear, you will do what I say or I will beat you into submission! You are a damned lucky girl to have the chance of marrying a Governor whatever he may be like, and you will show your gratitude by being pleasant to him.'

Denzil shouted the last words at her, then swallowed the wine that was in his glass, in one gulp before he went on, working himself up into a rage that she thought was even worse than those with which he had frightened her in the past.

'How dare you argue with me!' he stormed. 'How dare you discuss – suggest – you – an unfledged chick with no knowledge of the world – to whom you should or should not be married! It is I who will decide those things for you, and all you have to do is to obey me. And make no mistake, I intend to be obeyed! Do you hear?'

He roared the question at her and as if she could bear no more, Delora turned and ran from the room back to the bedroom where she had left her bonnet when she first arrived.

As she rushed she found to her relief, that Abigail was there. She flung herself against the old maid, holding onto her, as she said:

'Oh, Abigail .. thank God you .. are here!' and burst into tears.

It was after an uncomfortable luncheon, with Denzil grumbling and finding fault with the food which Delora found delicious after the restricted rations in the ship, that she went to lie down. When she did so, Abigail said:

'His Lordship will expect you to rest for at least two hours, M'Lady, as I hear he does himself. I'm going to slip down to the Admiral's House to see how the Captain is.'

'Oh, Abigail, can you do that?' Delora

cried. 'I intended to ask His Lordship if you might continue to look after the Captain, but he never gave me a chance, and I know, because he is angry with me, he would not agree to any suggestion I might make. In fact, he would be glad to refuse me.'

'Now don't you worry, M'Lady,' Abigail said. 'It's best to say nothing to His Lordship. You've upset yourself enough as it is, and if the Captain heard about it, he'd be worried about you.'

'Do not tell him .. please do not tell him!' Delora begged. 'There is nothing he can do .. and I do not wish him to quarrel with His Lordship.'

'I'll say nothing,' Abigail promised, and Delora knew she understood.

She felt as Abigail left her, that the old maid was the only thing left in her life which was solid and secure.

When two hours later Abigail came into her room, she sat up eagerly in her bed to ask:

'How is he?'

'He's a brave gentleman,' Abigail replied in a low voice. 'I've made him comfortable and his wounds, believe it or not, are better than I dared to hope they would be.'

'Oh, Abigail, I am so thankful!' Delora cried.

'Of course, the Captain was asking about you, M'Lady.'

'What did you tell him?'

'I told him you were being very brave.'

'Did he ask .. when I was to be .. married?'

'I couldn't tell him what I didn't know myself.'

Abigail busied herself getting Delora dressed in one of her pretty summer gowns, thinking as she did so, she had never known a gentleman suffer so intensely as the Captain, not physically, but mentally.

'It's a pity,' Abigail told herself, 'they can't be man and wife as nature intended.'

She knew that to say such things would not help either Conrad or Delora whom she had worshipped ever since she was a baby.

'Look after her,' Conrad had said, 'and if it is humanly possible, help her to bear what lies ahead of her.'

Abigail had heard the agony in his voice and knew he was thinking of what marriage to a man like Lord Grammell would mean.

Even in the short time he had been at Admiral's House people had talked to Conrad of the excesses and the outrageous behaviour of the Governor.

Other English Captains with ships in the harbour as well as officials in charge of the dock-yard had called at the Admiral's House as soon as Conrad had been brought ashore.

Deakin had entertained them while Barnet said fiercely that the Captain had done enough for one day and in fact, no-one was going to talk to him until he was stretched out in bed, which was a place he should never have left anyway.

It was only reluctantly, after Conrad in defiance of his usual very abstemious habits had drunk a glass of claret, that Barnet allowed his visitors, one by one, to have a few minutes with him.

The first was the Commander of a Brig who had got passed over in seniority even though he was older than Conrad. They had known each other for some years.

'It is good to see you, Horn, and your

reputation has preceded you. There is not a crew that comes out to this island which is not talking about you and your exploits. Nelson himself was not admired more.'

'You are making me embarrassed,' Conrad protested, 'but I am glad to see you, Forester. How long have you been here?'

'Nearly two months,' Commander Forester replied. 'My ship was practically sunk by a Privateer, but I was saved by an English ship which towed us into port. It will be another month at least before I can get to sea again.'

'In the meantime it is a pleasant island in which to have a holiday,' Conrad remarked.

'It could be, if it were not for the Governor!'

'Surely he does not interfere with you, or the dock-yard for that matter?'

'No, but I will tell you something that will make your hair stand on end...!' Captain Forester replied.

What he related made Conrad feel physically sick, not only with revulsion, but in fear for Delora.

When his other visitors told him almost

the same thing with various elaborations, he swore that somehow, but God knew how, he must save her, but he had no idea how he could do so.

That night he cursed his wounds for making him immobile, and yet at the same time he could not help being aware that if the *Invincible* or himself had not been wounded he might at this very moment, be making ready to sail away without realising the unbearable conditions in which he was leaving Delora.

His Excellency the Governor of Antigua, the Right Honourable Lord Grammell, arrived at Clarence House at five o'clock that afternoon.

He came there from St John's in an open carriage drawn by four horses and escorted by a troop of Cavalry.

He ignored the surly looks that he received as he drove along the beautiful road bordered on each side by trees and flowers, nor did he notice the exquisite view that was visible from every incline the horses reached or the red blossoms of the flamboyant which were a vivid contrast to the verdant green of the other trees.

He was, in fact, thinking with satisfaction of the amount of money he would receive on his marriage to the Earl of Scawthorn's sister.

'A good chap, Scawthorn!' he told himself with satisfaction. 'Since he has been here he has doubled the rate those Yankees have to pay me for trading on the island.'

The sun was still warm and as he neared Clarence House Lord Grammell thought of the wine that would be waiting for him.

He could never go for long without a drink, and he took the precaution of ensuring that every Captain who wished to ask him a favour brought with him a case of wine as an introductory opening to their conversation.

His escort turned in at the drive of Clarence House and the carriage came to a stop outside the stone steps which led up to the front door.

Lord Grammell negotiated the steps with difficulty owing to the fact that in the hot climate he took no exercise and his weight had increased since his arrival in Antigua.

He was panting as the sentries came to attention and he passed them without making any acknowledgement of their presence.

Denzil was waiting for him in the cool of the hall.

'It is good to see Your Excellency,' he said formally because he knew His Lordship enjoyed all the traditional pomp of his position.

'She has arrived – good! I was waiting for your message,' Lord Grammell said.

'And looking forward to meeting Your Lordship,' Denzil replied suavely.

As they entered the Drawing-Room the Governor said:

'You have told her we are to be married at once?'

'Yes, of course,' Denzil replied.

He held out a large glass of wine as he spoke, which Lord Grammell took from him and drank thirstily. Then he lowered himself carefully into an arm-chair and asked:

'What is all this I hear about a new two-decker in the harbour? And the Captain injured?'

'I expect you have been told he is a cousin of mine,' Denzil replied. 'Tiresome chap! It is a pity he was not killed!'

'Tiresome? Why tiresome?' the Governor's voice was sharp.

'It is all right,' Denzil replied. 'He is wounded and will be confined to a chair for sometime.'

'Thank God for that!'

'I was thinking,' the Earl said, 'it would be wise to be pleasant to him, not that it does not go against the grain to have to do so.'

'Why do you think that is necessary?'

'Well, he is inclined to be an interfering fellow like Nelson. You remember the trouble they had here with him?'

'I do because the damned idiots on this island never stop croaking about it,' the Governor said savagely.

Then in another tone of voice he asked:

'You really think this cousin of yours will make trouble?'

'He will if he gets to know too much. What I suggest is that we make ourselves agreeable.'

'In what way?'

'By sending him presents of wine, enter-taining him to dinner if he is well enough. Anything to keep him from being nosey.'

The Governor thought for a moment, then he said:

'You are right! Of course you are right! I will leave all the arrangements to you. And now let me see this little filly you have told me about.'

Delora had been sitting in her bedroom with Abigail waiting for the summons that she knew would come soon after she had heard the Governor arrive.

There was no need to tell the old maid she was frightened, and when a servant knocked on the door to inform her that her presence was required in the Drawing-Room, she gave a little cry that was almost inaudible, and yet to Abigail it was a scream for help.

'Now you behave as the Captain expects you to, M'Lady,' she said.

She knew she could not say anything that was more likely to give Delora the courage to face the man who was waiting for her.

She saw her chin go up and knew that her

beauty would appeal to any man, even to one about whom Abigail had already heard so much that she too felt like screaming.

Delora went through the door with her shoulders back and when she entered the Drawing-Room, while she felt everything was swimming before her eyes, she appeared quite composed, although her face was very pale.

Both Denzil and the Governor were sprawling in arm-chairs with glasses in their hands, and as Delora came into the room there was a perceptible pause before either of them moved.

Then with an effort Lord Grammell struggled to his feet and Denzil followed him.

'Present her!' he said almost sharply to Denzil, who his sister realised, was drunk, but making an effort to oblige.

'Lemme pres-ent, Your Exshellency,' he said, slurring his words, 'my sister, Lady Delora Horn, who'se delighted – yes, delighted, to make your acquaintance.'

Delora curtsied, then as she raised her head, it was only her breeding and the thought of what Conrad expected of her that prevented her from crying out aloud.

Never, she thought, had she seen a more repulsive man in her whole life.

His huge red and bloated face, a body puffed out and swollen with disease, a bulbous nose and thick sensuous lips made Lord Grammell look in appearance the monster he actually was.

His head was bald and the fat hand he outstretched towards Delora felt wet and sticky with the heat.

'My bride-to-be!' he announced in a thick voice. 'Welcome to Antigua, pretty lady! We will deal well together, you and I!'

His sharp eyes half-hidden by rolls of flesh seemed to Delora to look not only at her face but at her body, and she felt almost as if he undressed her.

Then as if with an effort at gallantry he raised her hand to his lips, and as she felt them touch her skin it was as if she shrank from the proximity of a reptile and one that was so poisonous that her instinct was to run away.

But she stayed her ground, her eyes very large in her face. Then having inspected her again, the Governor said:

'Sit down, sit down! You must tell me about yourself and your voyage here. Have a glass of wine.'

'N . no .. thank you,' Delora managed to say, thinking even to herself that her voice sounded strange.

'Nonsense!' the Governor replied. 'You need a drink! We all need a drink! What do you say, Scawthorn?'

'Of course!' the Earl replied.

He clapped his hands together, the door opened instantly and a servant came into the room.

He was a black man and elderly, and Delora suspected he had been at Clarence House for many years.

'Wine!' Denzil ordered briefly. 'Why the devil are you so slow with it?'

'It's here, M'Lord,' the servant replied as another man came into the room carrying a bottle wrapped in a white napkin.

'Fill up His Excellency's glass!' Denzil ordered, 'and bring another one for Her Ladyship.'

The glass appeared, the wine was poured

into it and Delora held it, not liking to refuse to drink it, but knowing she did not need it and feeling somehow that if she drank with these two men who had already had too much, she would become like them.

'I hear you were engaged in a battle on your way here,' the Governor said.

'Yes .. My Lord .. but one of the Privateers that was preying on four merchantmen was sunk .. and the other has been taken as a prize.'

'A Privateer sunk? Why was I not told of this?' Lord Grammell asked angrily.

He looked across at Denzil as he spoke and as if he realised that the information his sister had imparted was important he sat forward in his chair.

'Who sunk a Privateer?' he asked in drunken stupidity.

'The *Invincible* of course,' Delora replied, 'although they were very large ships, new and with better guns than anything the First Lieutenant had ever seen before.'

'And you say one was taken as a prize?' the Governor asked.

'Yes, Your Excellency. A crew from the

Invincible was put aboard and she was sent back to England.'

'You are noting that, I suppose, Scawthorn?' Lord Grammell said.

'There is nothing we can do,' Denzil replied.

'No, but it is unfortunate. I suppose the *Invincible* is bigger than anything we have had in these waters for a long time.'

'Much bigger,' Denzil agreed, 'and swifter!'

The Governor made an exasperated sound and sat back in his chair.

Delora looked from one to the other in perplexity.

She did not understand, but she felt perceptibly that what they had said was important and she must tell Conrad about it.

Then she wondered frantically, desperately, if there would be any chance of her seeing him, and if so – when?

Aloud she broke the silence by asking tentatively and in a very small voice:

'W . will Your .. Excellency tell me .. when you were .. anticipating we should be m .. married?'

CHAPTER SEVEN

'This is delicious, Barnet!' Conrad said, sipping from the long glass that he had just been handed.

'It's mango juice, Sir.'

'Then I could drink a bucketful of it.'

Sitting on the terrace outside the house with the sea lapping only a few feet from him and the sun shining through the leaves of the big trees, Conrad felt a surge of well-being sweep over him.

He knew it was due not only to the fruit, vegetables and fresh food he had eaten since he had arrived, but also that Abigail had been satisfied with his wounds when she had dressed them very early this morning.

She had crept out of Clarence House before anyone was awake and when she took off the old dressings she had ex-claimed with pleasure when she saw how cleanly the flesh was healing and that the

206

inflammation had gone.

'You are a good nurse, Abigail,' Conrad said.

'And you're a strong man, Sir,' Abigail replied.

'Another without your strength would have taken far longer to heal.'

Then, as if she had been too encouraging she said quickly:

'Now don't you go doing anything stupid, Sir. There's Her Ladyship worrying herself sick about you and the best you can do for her is to take things easy.'

'That is rather difficult at the moment.'

Conrad knew he did not have to elaborate to Abigail what he was feeling, and as if she knew what he wanted to ask her without having to put it into words, she said:

'His Lordship's intent on the wedding taking place in a few days.'

'What does Lady Delora say to that?' Conrad asked harshly.

'What can she say?' Abigail replied. 'She's always been frightened of His Lordship ever since she was a small child, and when he gets into one of his rages it's no use talking to him. He won't listen!'

She could feel the tension in Conrad's body as he wondered despairingly what he could do to help Delora or at least prevent this monstrous marriage from taking place.

Then because they were not questions he could ask Abigail he enquired:

'What is Her Ladyship doing today?'

'I think, Sir, she'll have a headache after being so long at sea, and we've already planned that I'll tell His Lordship after breakfast that she requires rest and quiet.'

Conrad gave a sigh of relief.

'That is wise.'

Yet he knew that if it did not suit his Cousin Denzil he would not allow Delora to rest but would force her to see Grammell and make herself pleasant, if that was what the Governor required.

Abigail had finished his dressings and she gave Barnet instructions as to what was to be done that evening if she could not get away to tend to Conrad herself.

'The Captain's to have plenty of fruit-juice,' she said. 'That's what he needs after a long voyage where everything began to taste like ashes in our mouths!'

Conrad laughed.

'You are not very complimentary, Abigail. We did our best on the *Invincible*.'

'I'm not saying, Sir, that you weren't obliging, and so were them as served under you, but I know what your body needs now, and it's up to Mr Barnet to see that you gets it.'

'I am sure Barnet will do that,' Conrad smiled, and Barnet had been bringing him glasses of fruit-juice all the morning.

Because Conrad loathed being in bed and also wished to discipline himself by getting onto his feet as quickly as possible, he insisted on being partially dressed and taken outside on the terrace so that he could not only be in the sunshine, but look at the sea.

The house which Nelson had occupied when he was in Antigua was very attractive with long French windows opening out of every room on the ground floor.

There was a terrace which was shadowed with cedar trees while huge clumps of hibiscus and poinsettia were patches of colour that somehow reminded Conrad of Delora.

He was sitting reading the newspapers, which were a month old but which he still found interesting, when he heard a carriage draw up outside.

With a little sigh he thought that more visitors had called to see him and he had hoped, after the crowd there had been yesterday, that he would have a little respite.

Then as he heard footsteps coming from the house he turned his head and to his surprise he saw a grossly fat man who he knew without being told, was the Governor, and behind him Denzil.

'His Excellency the Governor, Sir!' Barnet announced, 'and the Earl of Scawthorn!'

Conrad forced a smile to his lips.

'You must forgive me, Your Excellency, for being unable to rise and greet you.'

'No, no, of course not,' Lord Grammell replied. 'You must not exert yourself, but your cousin and I thought we should call and enquire after your well-being.'

'That is exceedingly gracious of you, My Lord,' Conrad replied politely. 'Good morning, Denzil.'

'Good-morning, Conrad! I am delighted

to see you in better health than I expected.'

'I am better, but it will take time,' Conrad replied.

'Of course, of course!' the Governor exclaimed. 'One cannot hurry nature. You must take things easily, Horn, like these damned niggers manage to do. They never exert themselves in the heat – they make sure of that!'

Conrad was not obliged to reply because Barnet, without being told, came from the house followed by a servant carrying a tray with glasses and drinks.

He had not thought that anyone would wish to drink wine so early in the morning, but the Governor apparently had no qualms about doing so while Denzil preferred rum.

They sat talking and Conrad had the impression that the Governor was anxious for the *Invincible* not to be repaired too quickly.

'You will find things very slow here,' he said in his thick voice. 'However much you take a whip to the niggers they will not work. I get complaints all the time about their indolence, but what can I do about it?'

'What indeed?' Conrad echoed as he had

no wish to make himself disagreeable.

At the same time he thought it would be impossible for any man to look so revoltingly debauched, so gross and unpleasant.

The Governor drank three glasses of wine before he came to what Conrad was sure was the point of his visit.

'Now listen, Horn,' he said, 'your cousin and I have a treat in store for you this afternoon, something I do not suppose you have seen before, even with your vast experience of visits to ports all over the world.'

'What is it?' Conrad enquired.

Lord Grammell put his finger up to his bulbous nose.

'That would be telling!' he said. 'It shall be a surprise! If you do not feel well enough to see it this afternoon, we could postpone it until tomorrow.'

'I feel well enough to do anything unless I have to travel any great distance,' Conrad answered.

'There is no question of that,' the Governor said. 'Where we are taking you is only a hundred yards or so from here. My men will carry you in the chair you are sitting in now.'

'You are making me curious, Your Excellency.'

'It will give you something to think about until we collect you at four o'clock,' the Governor said. 'In this climate we all need a *siesta* after lunch. Is that not so, Scawthorn?'

'Yes, indeed,' Denzil replied. 'You will find, Cousin, the place is like the dead between two and four.'

'A good way of describing it. Like the dead! Oh, well, that is what one person will be today anyway.'

He laughed again and Conrad wondered what he was talking about.

Then when his visitors had gone he wondered where they could be taking him and what he had to see.

He was puzzled by the Governor's remark about one person being dead, but could hardly imagine it would apply to himself.

At the same time, he was extremely suspicious at these overtures of friendship that were being made to him not only by the Governor but also by his Cousin.

He had not forgotten that Delora had said

213

that Denzil hated him because he was his heir.

Even so, he could hardly imagine that they were plotting to murder him, although he had learned by this time they had plenty of good reasons for doing so.

The Captains of the other ships in the dock-yard and the Naval Personnel living in Antigua had made it perfectly clear in one way or another what they suspected the Governor was doing.

They also said how ashamed they felt of his behaviour when the British were at war with the French.

Only the decisive defeat of Napoleon could bring peace to a world that was heartily sick of battles, and death, privation and suffering.

'Once you get the *Invincible* back to sea, Captain,' an officer had said, 'then you will have the chance of clearing up much of the treachery that is taking place around these shores. It prevents food from reaching England which I believe is vitally needed.'

'It is indeed!' Conrad replied.

His visitor had dropped his voice even

lower than it was already.

'They say because the English cannot pay the Governor as much as he wants they are not given the best stores when they come here to replenish their ships. In fact, they are often sent away without enough meat for the voyage ahead of them.'

Conrad felt his anger rising knowing that it was very easy for the Governor to say there were not enough cattle, sheep and pigs for a ship's requirements.

But if it sailed with empty holds, the men who were manning it suffered quite unnecessarily, once they were at sea, to the detriment not only of their health, but of discipline and fighting ability.

Having seen Grammell he realised how much he had deteriorated physically in the years that had passed since they had met at a Board of Enquiry. He could believe every story that was told about him, and a great many more besides.

Yet he told himself that for Delora's sake he must not antagonise either the Governor or Denzil, and he hoped by agreeing to anything they suggested that he would perhaps be asked to Clarence House where he could see her if only across a dining-room table.

The mere thought of her having even to talk to this monster, let alone do anything else, made him clench his hands together and long to hit something.

Then there was Barnet's voice announcing another visitor who came eagerly from the house with an outstretched hand to greet him.

Surprisingly after a good luncheon Conrad slept during the *siesta*.

He had expected to lie awake thinking of Delora. But he was more tired than he had realised, and when Barnet woke him he felt refreshed and knew that whatever the condition of his leg, his mind was alert and active.

'What I want to discover,' he told himself, 'is exactly what Grammell and Denzil are up to.'

He had already thought of ways by which he could send a secret report to the Admiralty if he found, as Nelson had done, that they were breaking the British Navigation Act.

He knew the difficulties of enforcing laws made in England when they were so far away, but it had been strictly laid down that 'the function of His Majesty's Ships of War was to protect the commerce of the nation', which in its turn meant ensuring that foreigners did not trade in areas where they were forbidden.

'I must manage to stop the Privateers somehow,' Conrad thought optimistically, 'but with the governor encouraging them and taking bribes from them, it is not going to be easy.'

He hoped his feelings towards Lord Grammell did not show when a little after four o'clock the open carriage in which he and Denzil were driving accompanied by their usual escort of Cavalry clattered up to the front door of the Admiral's House.

Denzil informed Barnet that they were driving on a little way down the road to the prison and four soldiers had been given orders to carry Captain Horn there.

When Conrad heard where he was being

taken he was surprised, but he said nothing and putting his cocked hat on his head, he allowed the soldiers to lift him.

Barnet, fussing like an anxious hen, gave them incessant instructions as to how careful they were to be, especially in carrying the support on which his leg rested.

He walked beside the chair, watching anxiously every step while Conrad looked about him interested to see how Antigua had altered since he had last been in these waters nearly fifteen years ago.

The prison was a small building which in peacetime did not have many inmates.

It was built surrounding a court-yard in the middle where he was carried to find the Governor and Denzil already there, seated on a platform against one side of it, which had an iron railing in front of it.

On Denzil's instructions the soldiers set Conrad down on the platform beside them, and while they did so, the Governor was in deep conversation with a man whose uniform proclaimed him to be a Prison officer.

Beside the soldiers who had carried

Conrad, there were four others armed with muskets standing on either side of the platform.

As Conrad stared out onto a patch of beaten-down sand he wondered what exactly was about to happen.

Then suddenly there was the baying of bloodhounds and when the heavy doors on the other side of the court-yard were opened Conrad could see six large dogs all jumping about behind iron bars.

He remembered he had heard that in the Southern States of America plantation-owners hunted any slaves who had tried to escape, with bloodhounds.

He could not believe that on an island the size of Antigua this was necessary, because if a slave ran away, where would he run to?

At the same time, the presence of the dogs made him uneasy and he looked at the Governor as if for an explanation.

His Lordship having finished his conversation, turned his head.

'Those are my dogs, Horn,' he said. 'I brought them with me from England. They have given me a lot of sport one way or another, but I am getting too old now to follow them on a horse. However they can still provide me with some amusement, and that is what you are going to see this afternoon.'

'See what?' Conrad asked.

Before the Governor could reply the prison-officers brought into the centre of the court-yard a negro heavily chained.

He was an enormous man, over six foot tall, with a magnificent body with highly developed muscles that made him look like a young Samson.

He was chained not only around his wrists but also his ankles. As he proceeded further Conrad could see that he had been flogged until his back was criss-crossed with weals, most of them raw and bleeding.

'You see that man?' the Governor asked. 'The strongest creature I have seen in my life! He can lift a tree out of the ground and smash it across his knees!'

'What crime has he committed?' Conrad asked.

'Oh, the usual ones,' the Governor replied blandly, 'disobedience, fighting and whoring. Well, those are things he will not do again!'

'Why not?'

Already Conrad felt a cold suspicion of what was going to occur.

'Flogging has only made him more defiant than he was already,' the Governor replied, 'and so he is going to be taught a lesson that he will not forget because he will not be alive to do so.'

Conrad drew in his breath.

'My little pets,' the Governor continued, mouthing the words above the baying of the dogs, 'have not been fed for forty-eight hours. They are hungry, Horn, and hungry animals can be very ferocious!'

Conrad felt the words of protest come to his lips, but he had lost the Governor's attention for Denzil was saying something on the other side of him.

'Yes, yes, of course,' Lord Grammell said, rising to his feet.

Then when both he and Denzil were standing he said to Conrad:

'Your cousin suggests we have a closer look at this man's muscles. They are amazing – absolutely amazing! He ought really to be stuffed and put into a Museum!'

Lord Grammell walked down from the platform as he spoke and a soldier opened a door in the iron railings which Conrad realised now was a protection against the dogs.

There was nothing he could do, but sit on the platform, tense and with tight lips and watch while the Governor and his cousin walked up to the huge negro who was standing quite still, staring at the blood-hounds.

As the Governor moved, two soldiers with muskets in their hands walked after him and as they stood to one side, Conrad could see by the expressions on their faces, they were admiring the negro in the same way that their master was doing.

Lord Grammell and Denzil were laughing together. Then the Governor gave an order and the chains were unlocked and taken away first from the negro's feet, then from his arms.

He was told to throw out the latter, then bring them in slowly so that the huge biceps above the elbow swelled in a manner that was quite remarkable.

Denzil said something which was undoubtedly obscene and the Governor laughed uproariously.

Conrad thought, watching the two men, that the expression on their faces was so revolting that it was even worse than the torture they envisaged for the man towering over them.

He was wondering what would happen if he shouted out that the whole idea was an outrage and something to which no man, black or white, should be subjected, in a civilised world.

Then as he felt that even for Delora's sake he would not be able to control the words which were rising to his lips, the negro made a sudden movement.

On the Governor's orders he had stretched out his arms once again so that he could bend them in slowly, making his muscles rise as he did so.

Then unexpectedly with a swiftness which was extraordinary in so large a man he brought his arms back and as he did so he reached out and clasped his great hands around the throats of the two men taunting him.

The movement was so quick that before Conrad or anyone else could grasp what had happened, he had bashed the Governor's and Denzil's faces against each other, not once but half-a-dozen times.

There was the sound of flesh slapping against flesh, of bones breaking while the force of the negro's movements made the blood spurt out over his victims' and his own body.

Then after what seemed an interminable time the bemused soldiers raised their muskets and shot the negro in the back. He fell forward crushing the bodies of his torturers beneath him.

His fingers were so firmly locked around their throats that it was to take several men a long time to force them apart...

Conrad signed the paper that lay in front of him and having sealed it with a wafer, handed it to the Naval Officer standing at his side.

'You will, Commander Beemish, carry this to the First Lord,' Conrad said, 'and inform His Lordship that I would be most grateful if he would convey its contents to the Foreign Secretary, Viscount Castlereagh.'

'I will carry out your orders, My Lord,' Commander Beemish replied. 'My ambition is to reach England in under twenty days.'

'With the new American frigate you captured yesterday I have no doubt you will succeed,' Conrad replied with a smile.

Commander Beemish grinned.

'It is very fortunate, My Lord, that she came into St John's harbour at just the right moment, having of course, no expectation that the Governor was dead.'

'Of course not,' Conrad agreed. 'At the same time, I have learned from the prisoners you took captive, that they have sunk or captured no less than six of our merchantmen in the last month!'

His voice was serious as he said:

'You know as well as I do, Beemish, that cannot be allowed to continue.'

'No, of course not, My Lord.'

'I have written fully to the First Lord telling him of the situation here,' Conrad said, 'and so that you shall be aware of what the report contains, I will tell you that I have been requested by the authorities in St John's and by the Naval Personnel on Antigua, to act as Governor until a replacement for Lord Grammell can be sent from England.'

'There is no need for them to be in a hurry,' Commander Beemish replied. 'When we heard you had agreed to do what was asked, every man in the dock-yard, including the crew of the *Invincible,* cheered themselves hoarse!'

'Thank you,' Conrad said simply.

'And may I, My Lord,' the Commander went on, 'add my good wishes and say that I am as glad as everybody else that the nightmare is over.'

Conrad was silent for a moment. Then he said:

'I think, Beemish, you will agree with me that in the best interests of Britain it would be wise not to say too much of what has been happening. They will have a pretty shrewd idea, but I can promise them that as long as I am here things will be cleared up and rapidly!'

'We all of us know that, My Lord.'

The Commander held out his hand and Conrad shook it.

'Good luck, Commander!' he said, 'and I hope you enjoy your voyage. I only wish I was coming with you.'

He spoke almost wistfully. Then as the Commander left Barnet came in to say:

'There's another visitor waiting to see you, M'Lord!'

The way he spoke brought a light to Conrad's eyes, and without waiting to be announced, Delora came running into the room.

She hardly waited until Barnet had shut the door before her arms were around Conrad's neck and her cheek was against his.

'I thought you would never be free!' she said. 'I am so jealous of all these people who take up so much of your time!'

'I am clearing the deck, my darling,' Conrad answered, 'so that when we get married in two days' time, I shall be able to have a honeymoon with you alone, without suffering from a guilty conscience.'

'Alone? Do you really mean alone?' Delora asked. 'Can we do that?'

'Am I, or am I not, at the moment, the Governor of this island?' Conrad asked.

Delora gave a little chuckle before she replied:

'You have become very important all of a sudden and I think, now you are an Earl and also a Governor, I am going to miss the brave but otherwise unimportant Captain, whom I used to dine with alone on board the *Invincible*.'

'I am important only because you love me,' Conrad said, 'and because although I can hardly believe it is true, you are going to be my wife!'

Delora gave a little cry.

'I, too, find it difficult to believe,' she said. 'Sometimes I wake up at night thinking the miracle has not happened, and I am to marry that horrible, ghastly old man!'

Conrad put his fingers against her lips.

'We agreed we would not talk about him,'

he said. 'As the Commander has just told me, the nightmare is over. Not only is Antigua free, but so are we, and we must not waste our minds and thoughts dwelling on what is past.'

'No, you are right,' Delora agreed. 'All I want to think about, darling wonderful Conrad, is you!'

He smiled at her, realising as he did so, that she had a new loveliness because she was so happy, and because although it seemed incredible they could now be married, as they believed God had always meant them to be.

Conrad in his usual decisive and authoritative way, had cut through all the red tape and the conventions that might have prevented their wedding taking place at what was certainly unprecedented speed.

One thing that had made it easy was that he had discovered that although it was known in England that he was taking Delora to Antigua to marry the Governor, it had not been announced on the island.

This made it easy for him to say that he and Delora had come to Antigua so that they could be married with the permission of her brother who was to have given her away.

The only thing that might have delayed their wedding was that Delora was in mourning, but he evaded criticism on this account by saying that it was imperative for her to be properly chaperoned.

The day after the Governor and Denzil had died, Conrad had arranged for Delora to stay with the wife of the Naval Officer in charge of the dock-yard.

She and Abigail had moved into their small house which was less than a hundred yards from where Conrad was.

Delora was so delighted at being nearer to him that she did not feel cramped, even though he was aware that her hosts were put to quite a lot of inconvenience to house her.

This provided another urgent reason why they should be married as quickly as possible, and he could think of no more attractive place for them to have a honey-moon than at Clarence House.

Delora had already described to him how beautifully it was furnished, and he knew that in his new position of authority he could give the order that they were to receive no visitors and that those who insisted on seeing him should be turned away at the gates, and they could find the flower-filled garden, the waving palms and flowery trees a Paradise all their own.

Although his injured leg was still lifted high on a stool beneath the writing-desk, he was feeling so well and so strong, he no longer thought of himself as an invalid. Now he said to Delora teasingly:

'You are quite certain you want to marry me? You realise I have never asked you formally.'

Delora gave a little laugh. Then she replied softly:

'I think actually I asked you! I know when Abigail came into my room to tell me that Denzil and the Governor were dead I exclaimed:

'"Now I can marry Conrad!"'

She bent forward as she spoke to kiss his cheek and he knew it was because she did not want him to see the tears of happiness that had welled up into her eyes.

There was no need to tell her that he had thought exactly the same thing, for he had no wish to speak of the horror of the mutilated blood-stained bodies lying in the court-yard of the prison or what they had looked like before they had been hastily buried that evening as was the custom in the tropics.

Now, as Delora had said shyly when she had come to see him the following day, all their dreams had come true.

'I suppose really,' she said tentatively, 'I ought to be worrying about your wounds and insisting on waiting until you are really well before I become your wife.'

'Abigail has said that I am well enough to be married,' Conrad answered, 'and you know perfectly well that we cannot argue with her!'

'I do not want to do so,' Delora replied, 'but I do not want to hurt you in any way. If you want me to, my darling, I will wait just as I was prepared to wait for years and years until we could be together as you promised we would be.'

'We are not going to wait one second

longer than we need,' Conrad said firmly. 'I would have married you tomorrow only I had first to see the Bishop. He intends to have the Cathedral massed with flowers, and apparently everybody on the island wishes to be present.'

'I would really .. like to marry you .. alone .. or perhaps .. aboard the *Invincible*.'

'That is what I too, would have liked,' Conrad agreed, 'perhaps even more than you would, because every woman enjoys a wedding. But I thought I should give Antigua something to think about, besides the behaviour of her last Governor, and when they have seen you, my beautiful, they will talk of nothing else!'

'I love you!' Delora replied, 'because you are not only so wonderful in every way, but you are so wise too. Oh, Conrad, will you go on loving me and wanting me, even when you leave me to go back to sea!'

There was a moment's silence. Then Conrad said:

'I have been facing facts, my darling, and I know that while in about six months time I may be well enough to undertake an arduous sea-voyage, I think it is unlikely I shall do so.'

He saw a sudden excitement creep into Delora's expression, and because he knew exactly what she was thinking, he said:

'First, I have a great deal to do at home in putting our affairs in order. I know from what you have told me and what I have heard, that Denzil neglected the family estates which must be restored to their past prosperity.'

'And then?' Delora questioned.

'Then I have the feeling, and I am almost sure I am not wrong, that the war will soon be over. We have to all intents and purposes, beaten Napoleon at sea. There now remains only a decisive battle to beat him on land, and I believe the Duke of Wellington will do that!'

Delora gave a little cry of happiness.

'Then you can leave the Navy and stay with me? It is the most wonderful, perfect thing that could ever happen. But darling, suppose I .. bore you?'

'You could never do that,' Conrad replied, 'but I have no intention of settling down so that I have nothing to do, except spend money whether it is yours or mine. I have a feeling there will always be a job waiting for me at the Admiralty, and apart from that I want to take my place in the House of Lords and fight for an improvement, not only in the ships that we must have to protect our shores, but in the treatment of our seamen.'

'No-one could do it better than you,' Delora cried.

'I have seen the appalling conditions in which men are prepared to fight and die for their country,' Conrad went on, 'and I am absolutely determined that something should be done for them.'

'And for the treatment they receive when they are wounded,' Delora said quickly.

'Naturally that is in my mind,' Conrad agreed, 'but I am afraid I cannot arrange that there should be two women called Delora and Abigail aboard every ship in the future!'

'But you can try to arrange that the Surgeons are more capable and are prepared to use other methods than the knife?'

'I shall never forget that it was you and Abigail who saved my leg,' Conrad replied. 'And I am prepared to dedicate a very large part of my life in the future to trying to see that other men are cared for as I have been.'

'You will let me .. help you?'

'You know I cannot do all these things without your love and without your inspiration.'

'That is what I want you to say,' Delora answered.

She pressed herself closer to him and she knew that no man could be so magnificent in every way, no man could make her feel when his lips touched hers, as if he carried her up into the sky and she was no longer human, but part of the divine.

She thought for one brief second of her unhappiness and fear when she had embarked on board the *Invincible,* which seemed now a century ago...

Then it had been cold and dark and because she knew where the ship must carry her, it made her feel as if she was journeying to an unutterable hell.

Yet from the very moment she saw Conrad

coming into the cabin she had felt as if he was enveloped by a light like a Knight going into battle and her whole life had been changed.

'I love you,' she said now, as he raised his head. 'I love you, and I pray every moment of the day that I shall make you the sort of wife you want, and one who is .. worthy of you.'

'You are not to talk like that, my darling one,' he answered. 'You are so perfect that I thank God that I am the most fortunate man in the world, because you love me.'

His lips were on hers again and he kissed her until the room vanished and they were both part of the sea and the sky.

Then she felt a warm wave that yet was a flame of fire, rising in her breasts which was so exciting and yet at the same time, part of the Glory of God.

She knew Conrad felt the same, and as he drew her closer and his heart beat against hers, the flame grew into a burning fire and yet she was not afraid.

His lips were fierce, passionate, demanding and she wanted to give him what he wanted, only she did not exactly know what it was.

She only knew she wanted him to go on kissing her. She wanted to be closer and still closer, to belong to him, so that they became one person and nothing could divide them.

Conrad released her lips to put his cheek against hers. Then holding her very tightly in his arms, he said in a strange voice:

'You excite me to madness, my darling, little love, but I promise that when we are married, I will be very gentle with you. I could never bear you to be frightened of me as you would have been with the man I brought you here to marry.'

'I could never be afraid of you,' Delora replied, 'and, darling, wonderful Conrad, I know that because I am very .. ignorant you have a great deal to teach me about .. love I want to learn .. I want to love you .. as you want me to and whatever we do .. it will be a part of God .. and part of .. Paradise.'

Her words made Conrad draw in his breath.

Then he was kissing her again, kissing her

passionately, but at the same time, with a reverence that he had never given another woman.

Delora had filled the shrine in his heart that had always been empty.

Now he knew she would be there always and for ever, and he would worship her because she had brought him the true, pure love for which all men seek as they voyage over the difficult, unpredictable and often tempestuous sea of life.

'I worship you,' he said against her lips.

Then there was no further need for words.

This Large Print Book for the partially sighted, who cannot read normal print, is published under the auspices of
THE ULVERSCROFT FOUNDATION